SCHOOL SPIRITS

Also by Rachel Hawkins

The Hex Hall series

Hex Hall

Demonglass

Spell Bound

SCHOOL SPIRITS

RACHEL HAWKINS

HYPERION

NEW YORK

First Edition
1 3 5 7 9 10 8 6 4 2
G475-5664-5-13060
Printed in the United States of America

Library of Congress Cataloging-in-Publication Data
Hawkins, Rachel, 1979–
  School spirits / Rachel Hawkins.—First edition.
      pages cm
  Summary: Fifteen-year-old Izzy, whose family has fought monsters for centuries, investigates a series of hauntings at her new high school.
  ISBN 978-1-4231-4849-4
  [1. Supernatural—Fiction. 2. Monsters—Fiction. 3. Magic—Fiction. 4. High schools—Fiction. 5. Schools—Fiction.] I. Title.
  PZ7.H313525Sc 2013
  [Fic]—dc22   2012046402

Reinforced binding

Visit www.un-requiredreading.com

SUSTAINABLE FORESTRY INITIATIVE   Certified Sourcing
www.sfiprogram.org
SFI-00993

THIS LABEL APPLIES TO TEXT STOCK

For Katie, the closest thing to a sister I have

CHAPTER 1

Killing a vampire is actually a lot easier than you'd think. I know movies and TV make it look really hard, like if you don't hit the right spot, it won't work. But the truth is, those are just rumors spread by vampire hunters to make themselves seem tougher. If everyone knew how easy it actually is to kill a vamp, there wouldn't be so many movies and TV shows and stuff. All it takes is a wooden stake and enough pressure to send it through the chest cavity. Doesn't really matter if you hit the heart or not.

See? So easy.

But capturing a vampire? Yeah, that's a little bit tougher.

"Just. Hold. Still," I mumbled around the tiny flashlight in my mouth. I was straddling the vamp's chest, my right hand holding a stake poised over his heart, my left clutching the little piece of paper with the ritual on it.

"Release me, mortal!" the vampire cried, but his voice broke on the last word, kind of ruining the dramatic effect. "My brothers will be here soon, and we will bathe in your blood."

I spit out the miniflashlight, and it landed on the hardwood floor with a clink. Pressing the stake closer, I leaned over him. "Nice try. We've been watching you for a week. You're working this town solo. No nest in sight."

"Nest" is what vampires call both their houses and the group of fellow vampires who are basically their roommates. I thought it was a pretty dorky name, but then, a lot about vampires is dorky.

This one was especially bad. Not only was he rocking the gelled hair, he'd moved into the one creepy, pseudo-Victorian mansion in town. He might as well have hung a neon sign blaring, HERE THERE BE VAMPIRE. All of his furniture was red velvet and heavy wood, and when I'd busted in earlier, he was in the middle of writing in a journal while a pretty blond girl sat near the fireplace.

She'd bolted when she saw me, and I was already cringing, thinking of how Mom would react to there being a witness.

The vampire, who was going by the name of Pascal, but was probably really a Brad or a Jason, twisted underneath me, but I was firmly seated. One of the perks of being a Brannick is that we're stronger than your average person. It also didn't hurt that this vamp was pretty small. When I'd wrestled him to the floor, I noticed that he was only a few inches taller than me, and most of that was his hair.

Sighing, I squinted at the piece of paper again. It was only a few words in Latin, but getting them right was important, and I'd never done this ritual by myself before.

That thought sent a bolt of pain through my chest, one I did my best to ignore.

Underneath me, "Pascal" stopped struggling. Tilting his head to the side, he watched me with his dark eyes. "Who is Finley?"

My grip tightened on the stake. "What?"

Pascal was still studying me, upper lip curling over his fangs. "Your head. It's full of that name. Finley, Finley, Finley."

Oh, freaking great. Vampires are a pain in the butt when they're just your garden-variety bloodsucker, but a few of them have extra powers. Low-level mind reading, telekinesis, that kind of thing. Apparently Pascal was one of the special ones.

"Get out of my head," I snarled at him, renewing my focus on the sheet of paper. "*Vado*—" I started, but then Pascal interrupted with, "She's your sister. Finley."

Hearing my sister's name from this . . . this *thing's* lips made the pain in my chest even worse, but at least no tears stung my eyes. I can't think of anything more pathetic than crying in front of a vampire.

Besides, if it were Finley here, if I was the one who was missing, she wouldn't have let a vamp, much less a vamp called *Pascal*, get to her. So I scowled down at him and pressed the stake hard enough to just break the skin.

Pascal drew in a hissing breath, but he never took his eyes off my face. "Nearly a year. That's how long this Finley has been gone. How long you've been working alone. How long you've felt like it was all your fau—"

"*Vado tergum,*" I said, dropping the piece of paper and laying my free hand flat against his sternum.

Pascal's gaze fell to my hand and he went even paler. "What is that?" he asked, his voice high with fear and pain. "What are you doing?"

"It's better than getting staked," I told him, but as the smell of burning cloth filled the air, I wasn't so sure.

"You're a Brannick!" he shrieked. "Brannicks don't do *magic*! What the hell is this?"

I kept up a steady stream of Latin, but *What the hell is this* was a totally valid question. The Brannicks had spent millennia staking vamps and shooting werewolves with silver-tipped arrows (and later, with solid silver bullets). We'd burned witches and enslaved Fae, and basically

4

became what monsters told scary stories about.

But things were different now. For starters, there were no more Brannicks besides me and my mom. Rather than hunt the Creatures of the Night, we worked for the Council that governed them. And they didn't call themselves monsters; they went by the much more civilized term "Prodigium." So the Brannicks were now more or less Prodigium cops. If one of their kind got out of hand, we tracked them, captured them, and did a ritual that sent them directly to the Council, who would then decide their punishment.

Yeah, it was a lot harder than just staking a vampire or shooting a werewolf, but the truce between Brannicks and Prodigium was a good thing. Besides, our cousin, Sophie, was a Prodigium, and set to be Head of the Council someday. It was either make peace or suffer some majorly awkward family holidays.

The ritual was nearly finished, the air around Pascal starting to shimmer slightly, when he suddenly shouted, "The boy in the mirror!"

Surprised, I sat back a little. "What did you just say?"

Pascal's chest was heaving up and down, and his skin had gone from ivory to gray. "That's what you're afraid of," he panted. "That he had something to do with Finley's vanishing."

My mouth had gone dry, and, blinking at him, I

shook my head. "No—" I started to say, only to realize too late that my hand had slipped off his chest.

Taking advantage of my distraction, Pascal gave another twist, this one stronger than the others, and managed to free one of his arms from beneath my knees. I was already ducking the blow, but the back of his hand caught me across the temple, sending me sprawling.

My head cracked against an end table, and stars spun in my vision. There was a blur of motion—vampires may not be that strong, but they *can* be fast—and Pascal was up the stairs and gone.

Sitting up, I winced as I touched my temple. Luckily, there was no blood, but a lump was already forming, and I glared at the staircase. My stake had rolled under the table, and I picked it up, curling my fingers around the wood. The Council may prefer for us to send monsters to them, but staking a vamp in self-defense? They'd be okay with that.

Probably.

I carefully made my way up the stairs, stake raised at shoulder level. The wall was lined with those tacky globe lamps—seriously, vampires are the worst—and a twinkling caught my eye.

Glancing down, I saw that I was covered in a fine layer of shimmery silver. Oh, *gross*. He was one of those body-glitter-wearing jerks. Now I was even more embarrassed that I'd let Pascal get inside my head, that I'd dropped my guard long enough for him to get away from me. If he got out of the house . . .

My fingernails dug into the stake. No. I was not letting that happen.

The landing was covered in burgundy carpet that muffled my footsteps. Directly across from me was a large mirror in a heavy gilt frame, and in it, I looked a lot less like a bad-ass vampire slayer and a lot more like a scared teenage girl.

My skin was nearly as papery white as Pascal's, a sharp contrast against the bright red of my braid.

Swallowing hard, I did my best to calm my hammering heart and racing mind. There was one thing vampires and Brannicks had in common: a few of us had special powers. Pascal's was reading minds, and mine—in addition to the strength and quick healing that came with being a Brannick—was sensing Prodigium. And right now, my Spidey senses were telling me Pascal had gone to the right.

I took one step in that direction.

On the one hand, my detection skills were dead on. On the other, I'd expected Pascal to be cowering behind a door or trying to open a window and get out. What I hadn't expected was for him to suddenly come barreling out of the darkness and slam into me.

We flew back onto the landing, crashing to the floor. I felt the stake tumble from my fingers, and with a grunt, tried to ram my knee up into Pascal's stomach. But this time, Pascal had the advantage—he was faster than me, and he'd caught me by surprise. He dodged my knee like it was nothing, and his fingers sank into my hair, jerking my head hard to the side and exposing my neck.

He was smiling, lips deep pink against the stark white of his fangs, and his eyes were black pools. Despite the stupid hair and the silly name and the flowing white shirt, he looked every bit the terrifying monster.

And when he ducked his head and I felt the sharp sting of his fangs piercing my skin, my scream was high and thin. This couldn't be happening. I couldn't go out like this, drained of blood by a dorky vampire calling himself *Pascal*.

A gray circle began to fill my vision, and I was so cold, colder than I'd ever been in my entire life. Then, from above me, there was a flash of silver, a glimpse of bright copper, and suddenly, Pascal was the one screaming. His body fell off of mine, and I raised a trembling hand to my neck, the rush of blood hot against my freezing skin.

Blinking rapidly to clear my vision, I scooted backward on the carpet, watching as the redheaded woman all in black dropped a knee in the middle of Pascal's chest, one hand pushing a bright silver amulet against his cheek.

Her other hand reached back and pulled a stake from the belt around her waist.

The stake swung down, and there was a sound almost like the popping of a bubble, and Pascal vanished in a surprisingly tiny cloud of dust and ash.

Head still swimming, I looked at the woman as she turned back to me.

Even though I knew it was impossible, I heard myself ask, "Finn?"

But the woman who strode over to me wasn't my sister.

"You okay?" Mom asked.

I pressed my palm tighter to the holes in my neck and nodded. "Yeah," I replied. Using the wall to brace myself, I went to stand up. As I did, my eyes skated over my mom, noticing that even though she'd been right on top of Pascal, she'd somehow managed to avoid getting even one speck of glitter on her.

"Of course," I muttered, and then the carpet was rushing up to meet me as I passed out at Mom's feet.

CHAPTER 2

The lights in our kitchen were too harsh. My eyes ached in the fluorescent glare, and my head was pounding. It didn't help that we'd taken an Itineris home. That was a type of magic portal, and they were located at posts all over the world. Problem was, like most things involving magic, there was a catch. While an Itineris made traveling a lot more convenient, it was also really rough on your body. I guess getting bent and twisted through the space-time continuum isn't exactly good for you.

The concoction in front of me finally seemed cool enough to drink, so I choked it down. It tasted like pine trees smell, but the ache in my head disappeared almost immediately. Across from me, Mom turned her coffee mug around and around in her hands. Her mouth was set in a hard line.

"He was a young vamp," she said at last, and I fought the urge to lower my head to the table.

"Yes," I replied, hand reaching up to touch the little puncture marks just under my jaw. Thanks to Mom's "tea," they were already starting to close, but they still hurt.

"He should have been no issue at all for you, Isolde," she continued, her gaze still on her mug. "I would never have sent you in there alone if I'd thought you couldn't handle it."

My hand dropped back to the table. "I could handle it."

Mom looked at the bite on my neck and raised her eyebrows. When she was younger, my mom had been beautiful. And even now there was something about the strong lines of her face that made people look twice at her. Her eyes were the same dark green as mine and Finley's, but there was a hardness that neither I nor my sister had.

"I mean, I *was* handling it," I mumbled. "But he was one of those mind-reading ones, and he . . . he got inside my head—"

"Then you should have shoved him right the heck out," Mom fired back, and I wondered what felt worse, the vampire bite or the guilt.

With a sigh, Mom dropped her head and rubbed her

eyes. "I'm sorry, Iz. I know you did the best you could."

But your best wasn't good enough.

Mom didn't have to say the words. I felt them hanging between us in the kitchen. There were a lot of words filling up the space between me and Mom these days. My sister's name was probably the biggest. Nearly a year ago, Finley disappeared on a case in New Orleans. It had been a totally routine job—just a coven of Dark Witches selling some particularly nasty spells to humans. We'd gone together, but at the last minute, Finley had told me to wait in the car while she dealt with the witches herself.

I could still see her standing under the streetlight, red hair so bright it almost hurt to look at. "I got this one, Iz," she'd told me before nodding at the book in my lap. "Finish your chapter." A dimple had appeared in her cheek when she grinned. "I know you're dying to."

I had been. The heroine had just been kidnapped by pirates, so things were clearly about to get awesome. And it had seemed like such an easy job, and Finley had swaggered off toward the coven's house with such confidence that I hadn't worried, not really. Not until I'd sat in the car for over an hour and Finley still hadn't come out. Not until I'd walked into the house and found it completely empty, the smell of smoke and sulfur heavy in the air, Finley's weapon belt on the floor in front of a sagging sofa.

Mom and I looked for her for six months. Six months of tracking down leads and sleeping in motel rooms and researching other cases like Finley's, and it all led nowhere. My sister was just . . . gone.

And then one day, Mom had just packed up our things and announced we were going home. "We have a job to do," she'd said. "Brannicks hunt monsters. It's what we do, and what we need to get back to. Finley would want that."

That had been the last time Mom had said Finley's name.

Now Mom sat across the table from me, and her coffee mug turned, turned, turned.

"Maybe we should take it easy for a while," she said at last. "Let you go on a few more missions with me, get your legs back under you."

Finley had been doing solo missions since she was fourteen. I was almost sixteen now, and this had been the first time Mom had let me out in the field by myself. I really didn't want it to be the *last* time, too.

I shoved my own mug. "Mom, I can do this. I just . . . Look, the vamp, he could read my mind, and I wasn't ready for that. But now I know! And I can be better on my guard next time."

Mom lifted her gaze from the table. "What did he see?"

I knew what she meant. Picking at the Formica table-top, I shrugged. "I thought about Finn for a sec. He . . . saw that, I guess. It just distracted me."

I didn't add the bit about how Pascal had mentioned the boy in the mirror. Bringing up Finn was going to bother Mom enough.

Just like I'd thought, her eyes suddenly seemed a million miles away. "Okay," she said gruffly, her chair shrieking on the linoleum as she shoved it back and stood. "Well, just . . . just go to bed. We'll think about our next move tomorrow."

Deep parentheses bracketed Mom's mouth, and her shoulders seemed more slumped than they had been just a few moments ago. As she passed my chair, for just a moment, Mom laid a hand on my head. "I'm glad you're okay," she murmured. And then, with a ruffle of my hair, she was gone.

Sighing, I picked up my cup and swirled the dregs of tea still left in it. Every bone in my body ached to go upstairs, take a shower, and crawl into my bunk.

But there was something I had to do first.

Our house wasn't much. A few bedrooms, a tiny kitchen, and a bathroom that hadn't been updated since the 1960s. Once upon a time, it had been the Brannick family compound. Back when there had been more

Brannicks. Now it was just a house surrounded by thick woods. But there was one room that really set it apart from your normal home.

We had a War Room.

It sounded cooler than it actually was. It was really just an extra bedroom stuffed with a bunch of boxes, a large round table, and a mirror.

It was the mirror I walked to now, yanking off the heavy canvas cover. Inside the glass, a warlock stared back at me.

His name was Torin, and he looked a couple years older than me, maybe eighteen or so. But since he'd gotten trapped in the mirror back in 1583, he was technically over four hundred years old.

"Isolde!" he called happily, leaning back, his hands on the table. "To what do I owe this lovely visit?" It was always bizarre watching Torin. Trapped in the mirror, he appeared to be sitting at the table in the middle of the War Room. But the actual table was empty. Even though I'd seen the phenomenon my whole life, I still caught myself glancing back and forth, as though Torin would magically appear on our side of the glass.

The thought made my head hurt all over again. In his own time, Torin had been an extremely powerful dark warlock. No one knew what spell he was attempting when he'd trapped himself inside the mirror, but one of my ancestors, Avis Brannick, had found him and taken responsibility for him.

The fact that Torin made the occasional prophecy had probably had something to do with that. His ability to see the future had come in handy for a few Brannicks over the years; easier to fight a witch or a faerie when you know what it's going to do.

But I hadn't come to have my fortune told. Climbing up onto the table, I crossed my legs and propped my chin in my hand. "I got bitten by a vampire tonight."

Frowning, Torin leaned forward. "Oh," he said, once his eyes settled on the bite mark. "So you did. That . . . What is the word you use?"

I couldn't help but smile a little as I rolled my eyes. "Sucks."

Torin nodded. "Even so." He mimicked my pose, ruby pinkie ring flashing in the dim light. Shaggy blond hair fell over his forehead, and when he smiled at me, his teeth were just the slightest bit crooked. "Tell me the whole story."

So I did, the way I always had, ever since I was old enough to go with Mom and Finley on missions. There was something . . . I don't know, relaxing about telling the story to Torin. I knew he wasn't looking for all the flaws in my mission, all the places where I had zigged when I should have zagged.

Unlike Mom, Torin didn't frown through the entire thing. Instead, he chuckled when I described Pascal's lair, grimaced when I mentioned the body glitter, and raised his eyebrows when I talked about chasing the vamp up the stairs.

"But you're all right. And you lived to fight another day."

Sighing, I pulled my braid over my shoulder, fiddling with the ends of my hair. "Yeah, but if Mom hadn't come in . . . She thinks I shouldn't be doing jobs on my own. Which, I mean, I should. This one got a little out of hand, but if she'd just trust me a little more—"

"If she had trusted you completely, she wouldn't have followed you, which means she wouldn't have burst in when she did," Torin said, lifting his shoulders. "And you, my lovely Isolde, would either be exsanguinated on what I can only guess was truly dreadful carpet, or the bride of the undead." He narrowed his eyes. "Neither fate suits you. Or me, for that matter."

His words seemed to lodge somewhere in my chest, but I shook them off. Torin had been a part of my life for, well, all of my life. When Mom and Finley had gone out on missions, he had kept me company. And after Finley disappeared, he was the only one I could talk to about my sister. Which is why that niggling suspicion, the one Pascal had picked up on, bothered me so much.

17

"Your mum is simply worried about you," Torin said, pulling me out of my thoughts. "She's lost one daughter. I'm sure the idea of losing another is particularly hellish for her."

"I know," I said, the guilt returning with a vengeance. What if I'd gotten myself killed tonight, all because I let one stupid vamp mess with my mind? Where would Mom have been then?

I tugged the rubber band off the end of my braid and started unraveling the strands. A thin layer of vampire ash rose from them. Ugh. Apparently I'd been closer to Pascal than I'd thought.

Wrinkling my nose with disgust, I hopped off the table. "Okay. Shower, bed. Thanks for the debriefing."

Torin made a little flourish with his hand, lace cuff falling back from his wrist. "Any time, Isolde."

I was nearly to the door before I turned back. "Torin, you . . ." I trailed off, not sure how to finish. Finally I took a deep breath and said, a little too fast, "You swear you don't know anything about Finn, right?"

I'd asked it before, the night Finley disappeared. Other than her belt, there'd been no sign of my sister in that rickety house. But there had been a mirror. A big one with a thick wooden frame, carved cherubs grinning at me. And while it could've been a trick of the light, I could've sworn that the glass had glowed slightly.

But I'd been beyond freaked out that night, confused, upset. I couldn't be sure what I'd seen, really.

In his mirror, Torin came up close to the glass. "No, Isolde," he said, his voice surprisingly gentle. "I do not know where your sister is."

"Right." I ran a hand through my hair, blowing out a long breath. "Right. Okay." Reaching out, I flicked off the switch.

From out of the darkness, Torin added, "Besides, Finley was never of much interest to me. She isn't the Brannick who will set me free, after all, is she?"

It was a wonder I could speak given how tight my throat had gone. "That's never going to happen, Torin. I may be nicer to you than my mom or Finn, but you'll be chatting with my *grandkids* from that mirror."

Torin only laughed. "I've seen what I've seen. The time will come when you will finally let me out of this cursed glass prison. But until then, go wash that vampire out of your hair and get a good rest. You and Aislinn will be taking quite the journey tomorrow."

"Where are we going?" I demanded. "What did you see?"

But there was no answer.

CHAPTER 3

When I woke up the next morning, Mom was already dressed and waiting for me at the kitchen table. She frowned at my tank top and pajama pants and pointed back up the stairs. "Get dressed. We're leaving in five minutes."

"Leaving?" The clock said it was just a little past six. Apparently Torin had been right. I rubbed the sleep from my eyes. "Where are we going?"

But Mom just said, "And now it's four minutes. Go."

There wasn't much to the bedroom Finley and I had shared. A bunk bed—Finn had claimed the top—a dresser, a battered desk, and a mirror. Finley's clothes were still folded in the drawers, and almost without thinking, I grabbed one of her black sweatshirts, tugging it over my tank top. I traded my flannel pants for jeans (my own, since Finn had been taller than me), and added a scuffed pair of black boots.

Jogging back downstairs, I twisted my hair into a sloppy braid over one shoulder. Hopefully, wherever we were going didn't have a dress code.

Mom was just outside the front door, and when I appeared at her side, she didn't say anything, merely jerked her head toward the woods surrounding the compound. Years ago, all the Brannicks had lived in this secluded spot deep in the woods of northern Tennessee. There were still outbuildings and training yards to accommodate at least a hundred people, but I'd never seen the place that full. By the time I was old enough to remember, the only Brannicks left were me, Mom, and Finn.

The woods were full of noise that morning, from the cracking of branches under our feet to the birds singing, but Mom didn't say anything and I didn't ask any questions.

Nearly a mile into the trees, we came to the Itineris. To anyone walking by—not that many people ever just "walked by" in these woods—the portal wouldn't have looked like anything but a small opening in a bunch of branches. They wouldn't even know it was there unless they accidentally stepped into it.

Which would probably be fatal since the Itineris was

too intense for humans. We could only use it because we had some residual magic in our blood.

Mom held out her hand to me, and I took it, ducking under the branches and stepping into the Itineris.

One of the weirdest things about using the Itineris is how it feels. There's no rushing wind or sense of motion, but a crippling, sickening pressure, as though the weight of the whole universe is pressing down on you.

Suddenly, we were standing on a paved road.

Well, Mom was standing. I was on my knees, gasping. The portal was always rough on me.

Mom helped me to my feet, but that was clearly all the TLC I was going to get. As soon as I was steady, she started walking down the road.

"Where are we?" I asked, following.

"Alabama," she replied.

I didn't ask what part of Alabama, but between the sand and the slight tang of salt on the wind, I guessed we were somewhere near the beach. We hadn't been walking long when we came across a path of crushed shells. Mom turned onto it, her boots crunching and sounding too loud in the quiet.

At the end of the driveway was a small, one-story house that actually looked a little bit like our place. An ancient Jeep was parked just by the front porch, and several sets of wind chimes twisted in the breeze.

The screen door creaked open, and a woman stepped out, squinting down the drive at us. She seemed to be about ten years or so older than my mom, and her dark blond hair, shot through with gray, was piled on top of her head in a messy knot. Her arms, bare in a black tank top, were pale and flabby. Roughly a dozen necklaces and pendants hung around her neck, and she held a coffee cup in her right hand. "Ash?" she asked, frowning at us.

"Maya," Mom returned. She gestured at me. "Mind if me and Izzy come in for a bit?"

Maya glanced over, seeming to notice me for the first time. I raised my hand in a tiny wave. "Hi."

Maya didn't wave back, but sighed and said, "Too early in the morning for Brannicks." Then she turned and walked back into the house.

I dug a little hole in the shells with the tip of my boot. "Does that mean we should go?"

To my surprise, Mom just chuckled. "No. If Maya hadn't wanted us here, trust me, she would have let us know."

"Who is she?" I asked, but Mom didn't answer; just trudged up the steps and into the house.

And after a long moment, I followed.

The house wasn't quite as spartan as our place, but it still wasn't what anyone would call homey. No pictures lined the walls, although Maya did have one of those crazy cat clocks, the swinging tail marking off seconds, its eyes darting back and forth like it was watching for something. The only other things of note were a sagging couch covered in an ugly orange-and-brown plaid and a crooked coffee table. But that wasn't what had me freezing in the doorway. Instead of magazines or heavy books, the coffee table was covered in . . . feet. Not human feet—at least I didn't *see* any—but half a dozen chickens' feet, several of those rabbit's foot key chains, and a brown, furry paw. Char marks dotted the table's scarred surface, and there was a cracked leather book lying open facedown, its pages wrinkled. Everything about it screamed magic, but I hadn't sensed anything when we came in, so I didn't think Maya could be Prodigium. Maybe she was just a . . . taxidermist or something. Mom had made some weird friends over the years.

And she must've been here before, because she didn't even blink at the bizarre collection. But she did lean in and whisper, "Don't say anything until I tell you to, okay? And don't take anything Maya gives you to drink."

I tried very hard not to gulp. "Got it."

Sure enough, Maya came out of the kitchen holding three mugs, steam rising off of them. Even across the room, the smell turned my stomach. Still, Mom accepted two cups before sitting on the couch. I sat next to her as

Maya took a seat on the floor in front of the coffee table. She was wearing a long skirt, and it jangled softly when she moved, as though there were bells hidden in its folds.

"So you're Izzy," she said, blowing the top of her drink. "Your mama brought Finley here plenty of times, but she always said you were too young to go out on jobs. How old are you now, thirteen?"

I had always looked younger than I was. "I'll be sixteen next month," I told her, and she gave a low whistle. "My, my, time is flying. When I first met you, Ash, Izzy was what? Five? Maybe six? It was right after her daddy died, and—"

"We didn't come here to chat, Maya," Mom broke in. "I wanted to go through the file."

Maya rolled her big blue eyes. "That's it? You could've e-mailed, you know. You didn't have to hike all the way out here for that kind of thing. I thought at the very least you wanted another locator spell. See if we'd have any luck finding your girl this time."

25

CHAPTER 4

With that, she rose to her feet and went back into the kitchen. While she pulled things out of cabinets and drawers, I leaned closer to Mom. "A locator spell? For Finn?"

"Hush, Izzy." She said it calmly, but her shoulders were stiff, and she was bouncing one foot up and down.

"She's a *witch*?" I hissed. "You went to a witch looking for Finn and you never told me?"

"It was none of your business." Mom's voice was sharper now, her hands digging into her thighs, and I jerked my head back like she had slapped me. To be honest, I kind of felt like she had.

Then Mom sighed and leaned closer to me, her voice softer as she said, "Iz."

I shook my head, biting off anything clsc I wanted to

ask about Finn. Instead, I said, "I couldn't feel her. Maya. And I can always sense witches."

"I'm a *hedge* witch," Maya said, coming back into the living room holding a folder overflowing with paper despite all the rubber bands wrapped around it. "Which is why your mother is insulting me greatly by using me to gather this sort of stuff." She waved the folder a little, and few Post-it notes fell out.

"What's in there?" I asked, and Maya sighed, pulling the rubber bands off the folder.

"Articles, weird things that popped up on the Internet . . . Basically, I keep an eye out for any news story that seems to involve the supernatural."

I turned to Mom. "This is how you find cases?"

Mom had never looked sheepish in her life, I was willing to bet, but something really close to that expression crossed her face now. "Not always. But sometimes it makes sense to . . . outsource."

I knew Mom had friends who helped her out on cases from time to time. There was the guy who got her the boat when she had to find those killer mermaids, and we always seemed to have plenty of money that came from some mysterious source. But a middle-aged lady in the middle of nowhere collecting articles about possible supernatural happenings? That seemed kind of . . . lame.

As Maya sat down in front of the coffee table, I pulled

the sleeves of my shirt over my hands and asked, "What's a hedge witch?"

Clearing all the feet away, Maya opened the folder. "The kind of witches you're used to are born that way. What is that stupid word they have for themselves?"

"Prodigium," Mom and I answered in unison.

"Right, well, Prodigium come into their powers at what, twelve? Thirteen? And they can just do magic. No wands, no spell books necessary unless they're trying to do the super-dark crap. Point is, it's an inborn ability." Maya began paging through the papers. Some were newspaper articles with big garish headlines. I spotted one that blared, SEA MONSTER SPOTTED AT NEW ENGLAND RESORT!

"Now, it strikes me that this is incredibly unfair," Maya continued. A pair of glasses dangled from a beaded chain around her neck, and she picked them up, balancing them on the end of her nose as she continued to scan the papers. An article that seemed to be about crop circles drifted to the carpet.

"Why should some people be born gods while the rest of us poor mortals have to struggle through the mud of humanity, trying—"

"Enough, Maya." Mom turned to me. "A hedge witch is someone who can do magic, but they've learned it from books. And their abilities are severely limited compared to natural witches."

"I resent the term *hedge witch*," Maya said with a haughty lift of her shoulders. "What I do is every bit as natural as what fancy Latin witches can do. If anything, hedge magic is more elegant."

I glanced at the little pile of feet on the carpet and bit back a sarcastic comment.

"Ah," Maya said at last, pulling out a large piece of paper. "Here's the one I was looking for. Caught my eye because it happened so close by."

She handed it to Mom, and I leaned so that I could read it over her shoulder. It was a photocopy of a newspaper piece. There was a grainy photo of a stretcher being pulled out of a large brick building, police tape everywhere. The caption read, STILL NO LEADS IN ATTACK ON POPULAR TEACHER.

"What happened?" I tapped the picture.

"Was just a few months ago," Maya said. "I remember it because that town in Mississippi was close enough to here that it made the local news. The science teacher was found nearly dead from a blow to the head."

"Okay, well, that seems awful but not necessarily supernatural," I said, but Mom shook her head. Pointing to a section of the article, she said, "Read this part. 'Police are particularly baffled as David Snyder was found in a room *locked from the inside*.' No witnesses, no fingerprints. And he swears he was alone in the room."

29

I read all of that, but I still didn't get it. "It's creepy, but it still isn't all that Brannick-y."

Mom looked up at me, the corners of her mouth turning down. "Unless it's a haunting."

Digging my fingers into the couch cushions, I tried very hard not to roll my eyes. "Mom, come on. A *ghost* case?"

As far as Supernatural Threats went, ghosts were way down there at the bottom of the list. For the most part, they just floated around and creeped people out, and they were ridiculously easy to banish.

But Mom actually smiled. "This sounds perfect, Iz. Exactly the kind of case you could tackle by yourself, get your confidence back—"

Now I couldn't keep the petulance out of my voice. "Mom, ghosts jobs are nothing. They're . . . they're like Brannick training wheels."

"Tell that to Mr. Snyder," Maya muttered, and Mom nodded.

"If this is a haunting, it's a potentially dangerous one. We owe it to the students of"—she squinted at the paper—"Mary Evans High to keep them safe."

Flipping my braid over my shoulder, I sank deeper into the couch. "I know, but—" I sat up straight. "Wait, this happened at a high school?"

Mom had always gone out of her way to avoid jobs that happened at schools. She'd never said why, but

I'd guessed it had to do with me and Finn and Mom not wanting us to get any ideas about a "regular life." That's why we'd always been homeschooled, although I doubt many kids had to write an essay on *The Hammer of Witches* as their midterm. And sure, a few years ago, I'd kind of . . . not longed for it, exactly, but I'd thought high school had a certain exotic appeal. But that was when I was just a kid.

Whatever was on that piece of newspaper suddenly became very interesting to Mom, and dread began to settle in my stomach. "Mom, is this . . . am I going to have to go to this high school?"

Mom didn't look up. "It would be the best way for you to do the necessary reconnaissance work. And it might be good for you." Her mouth tightened into a firm line, and I knew that whatever came out of her mouth next, it would be a command, not a request. "This is the case for us right now, Isolde. The case we need."

When Mom used that voice, there was no arguing. It was the same tone she used to get me to put in an extra hour on the training field.

The same tone she used the day she'd said we were done looking for Finley.

"Yes, ma'am," I said, hoping I didn't sound sullen. But . . . high school. Regular high school, with . . . with . . . Yeah, I had no idea what that would actually entail, other than a vague notion of school dances and lockers. And while our cabin in the woods may not be much, it was home.

"The town is only about fifty miles from here," Maya offered. "I could ride with y'all, show you around." She narrowed her eyes at Mom. "And I'm assuming you have ways of finding a place once you get there."

"I'll make some calls," Mom said tersely.

"We won't need a *place*," I insisted, rising to my feet. "*Places* are for jobs that are more than chasing down Casper."

Mom began gathering the pieces of paper. A few caught her eye, and she folded them carefully, putting them in the pocket of her jacket. "Enough, Iz."

She stood up and said to Maya, "We'll need to go home, get a few things first. We'll drive down next week."

I frowned at that. We had a car, but it was not the most reliable thing, and as much as I loathed Itineris travel, it was a lot faster.

While Mom and Maya made plans, I sat back on the couch, the newspaper article in my hand. I knew I should have been more concerned about the guy being pulled out on a stretcher, but my gaze kept going again and again to the big brick building behind him. Mary Evans High.

A shiver went through me, and I was pretty sure it had nothing to do with any ghost.

CHAPTER 5

"I'm so glad you could finally join me, Isolde," Torin said, smiling as he crossed a large gilded room. He was wearing a fancy suit of emerald-green velvet rather than his usual outfit of black pants and white shirt, so I knew I was dreaming.

Again.

"I told you, no dreams," I said, but he just shrugged.

"Yes, but that was ages ago."

"It was two weeks ago," I countered, even as I took the golden goblet he offered me. My hand glittered with rings, and the dress I was wearing was so heavy I wanted to sit down. "And if memory serves, I've been telling you to cut out the dream-walking thing for the past five years." I smoothed my skirt. "Why can I never wear my regular clothes?"

Torin sipped his own drink. "My world, my dress code. Besides, you look lovely."

There were never any mirrors in these dreams, so I had to take his word for it.

"Was this your house?" I asked. Liveried servants lined one wall, holding trays with more goblets. Music was playing somewhere nearby, but I couldn't quite pin down the song.

"Free me, and you can see for yourself."

Scowling, I handed him back his cup. "That's never happening. No matter how many times you invade my dreams to play dress-up."

He took my hand in his, and I was surprised by how warm his skin was. Torin had never touched me in these dreams before. "I'm simply trying to show you that I'm not all bad. That freeing me will not unleash some sort of plague onto the world. This is all I want," he said, nodding at the room. "My old life back."

I jerked my hand from his. "Your 'old life' ended nearly half a millennia ago. This"—I waved a bejeweled hand— "doesn't exist anymore. Outside of rap videos, at least."

Torin leaned against the wall with an extravagant sigh. "You make me sad, Isolde."

"And you bug me. Now get out of here and let me dream about . . . I don't know, whatever it is normal teenage girls dream about."

Turning his head, Torin studied me. His eyes were green, like mine, but whereas mine were shot through with gray, his had flecks of gold, like a cat's. Or maybe they were just reflecting all the gilded crap in the room. "Do you even know how to be a normal teenage girl?"

I backed up, wobbling in my brocade dress. "I guess I'll figure it out, won't I?"

His grin was slow and lazy. "Indeed. And speaking of—"

The room began to fade, and another voice said, "Here you go."

Something landed in my lap, jolting me out of sleep.

Mom was sliding into the driver's seat of the car, and I rubbed my eyes. That's right. I wasn't in a sixteenth-century ballroom. I was in the parking lot of a Walmart. I felt the dream curling around me, but I shook it off as I sat up, inspecting the bag Mom had tossed at me.

"I got everything they had that was set in high school," she told me, starting the car.

Reaching into the bag, I pulled out several boxed sets of TV shows. I held up one, making a face. "Um, Mom, unless regular high school involves me having to avenge the murder of my boyfriend's identical twin who turns out to actually *be* my boyfriend, I don't think this is going to be a huge help."

"Better than nothing."

The car sputtered and lurched as Mom turned onto the highway, and I fought the urge to ask why we couldn't have gotten a new car for this job.

Mom had managed to find us a tiny rental house in the tiny town of Ideal, Mississippi. Maybe the town founders had called it "Ideal" as a joke. Other than a few strip malls and neighborhood after neighborhood of houses exactly like ours, Ideal didn't have that much to offer.

Except for a high school that may or may not have a major-league haunting going on.

We pulled into the driveway of our house. Like the house on either side of it, it was covered in beige vinyl siding, and while it was definitely a step up from the cabin, it was still depressing.

I helped Mom lug the rest of her purchases in, and was about to head up to my room to watch my brand-new TV shows on my brand-new television when Mom stopped me.

"Should we . . . Do you want to go back and get you some new clothes? I didn't even think about that."

My entire wardrobe consisted of black jeans, black T-shirts, and a selection of hoodies. Those were black, too, except for the pink one Finn had once gotten me as a joke. "I'll be fine," I told her. I'd seen enough kids to know that, while I wouldn't exactly be a supermodel, I wouldn't look like a total freak, either.

Mom nodded. "Okay. What about your cover story? Should we go over that one more time?"

I just barely managed to keep from rolling my eyes. We'd been over my cover story at least half a dozen times on the drive from Tennessee to Alabama, and then again on the drive from Maya's to here. I could have recited it in my sleep. The gist of it was that I was Izzy Brannick— Mom let me use my real name since this was my first time doing a case solo—and I was from Tennessee. My mom had taken a job in the next town over, but we moved to Ideal because the schools were better. Short, simple, sweet.

Still, I repeated it to Mom. When I was done, she seemed satisfied, although I had a feeling I'd have to do it again before school tomorrow. "Anything else you want to talk about?" Mom asked, and I shook my head.

"You good for the rest of the night?" Mom was already glancing down the stairs.

"Sure," I told her. "Go . . . do your thing."

Mom's "thing" was locking herself in the spare bedroom and poring over books and journals and weird magical documents. I wasn't sure if she was searching for something that would help us on this case or just boning up on her General Monster Research. And there was that little part of me that wondered if she was looking for clues about Finn, but I never asked. I didn't even know where any of that stuff had come from. It had just started showing up at the house right after we moved in last week. From more of Mom's "friends," I guessed.

Once I was in my room, I sorted through the DVDs, trying to decide which one to watch first. The one with the girl who falls in love with an alien sounded the most interesting, but I figured it, like the *Secret Twin Murder Show*, wouldn't be that useful. So in the end, I picked the show about the poor girl who transfers to the rich-kid high school, *Ivy Springs*.

The cover was pretty boring, but by episode three, I was so into it that I didn't even notice Torin in my mirror until he cleared his throat. Frowning, I reached out and clicked pause right before Everton, the rich boy, told Leslie, our impoverished heroine, that he had feelings for her. "What?" I snapped at Torin.

"Just checking in on you. You could be a little thankful, you know. Getting out of my own mirror requires considerable power on my part."

"First of all, no, it doesn't," I countered. "You zip in and out of those things all the time. And secondly, I would be thankful if I wanted to talk to you, but I don't, so I'm not." I had too much on my plate right now to deal with Torin. Especially since I was still irritated about the dream invasion.

"That is unkind," Torin sniffed. In the mirror, he

was sitting on my bed. Mom had let me pick out a new bedspread yesterday, but I'd been so overwhelmed by all the patterns and the flowers and the pop stars that I'd ended up picking a plain green blanket that looked almost identical to the covers I'd left behind.

Ignoring Torin, I started the show up again. Everton confessed his love, Leslie swooned, and just as they were about to kiss, Torin piped up, "Those two seem insipid."

I shot a look at him. "Shut up."

"I mean it. And doesn't that lad have another girl? This can really only end badly for everyone involved."

In spite of myself, I smiled a little. "I guess I should get used to this kind of drama."

Torin smiled back. "Certainly scarier than staking vampires, isn't it?"

I wondered what it said about me that watching a teen soap opera with a four-hundred-year-old warlock felt, well . . . normal.

"I don't know why I'm doing all of this," I said, not taking my eyes off the screen. "Or why Mom is going to all this trouble. If there's a ghost here—and I kind of doubt it—it won't require my going to this school for, like, months or renting a house. We could just get in, get out—"

"Isolde, do not be so dense." In the mirror, Torin

was leaning back on his hands, ankles crossed. "Your moving here has nothing to do with any ghost. Granted, there's a chance a haunting is happening at Betty Crocker High—"

"Mary Evans," I corrected, but he blew a hank of blond hair out of his eyes and shrugged.

"But clearly, Aislinn's true motivation here is to let you experience a taste of regular human life. She's gruff and difficult, that woman, so of course she'd rather die than tell you, 'Oh, Isolde, guilt over your sister's disappearance has left me swimming in a veritable sea of angst—'"

"Stop it." Standing up, I flipped off the television and turned to face Torin. "Just . . . if you can't help with Finley, then don't talk about her, okay?"

Torin pursed his lips slightly, tilting his head and studying me. Then he said, "I did not mean to offend. I simply wanted to make sure you understood why you're really here, Isolde. This isn't about hunting a ghost. It's about your mum trying to do something for you that she never did for your sister."

Snorting, I headed for the door. "Mom doesn't think like that."

"I've known her longer than you have," Torin called, and I froze, hand on the doorknob. I'd never really thought of it like that, but yeah, Torin had been in our family for centuries. He'd seen Mom grow up. Had known my grandmother, my great-grandmother, all the Brannicks stretching back to the sixteenth century.

Leaning forward, Torin gave his best sheepish smile. "Now, can we please stop quarreling and finish this program? I really do want to see what fresh hell is unleashed next."

I hesitated, and Torin clasped his hands on his knees, sitting up straight. "I promise to behave."

Somehow, I doubted that, but to be honest, I really wanted to see how that episode went. So I settled back on the floor and turned the TV on. Leslie and Everton kissed, his girlfriend found out, and the episode ended with Leslie running down the street in tears while some seriously whiny music wailed in the background.

"Well," Torin said as the credits began to roll, "take heart, Isolde. At least a ghost will be less terrifying than *that*."

CHAPTER 6

The next morning, I woke up before my alarm. It wasn't like I'd never thought about the first day of school before. I remembered going into stores with Mom and Finn, passing all those displays of pencils and binders and backpacks, and wondering what it must be like to live that kind of life. But I'd never thought that would be my life.

I was still brooding when I headed downstairs and into the kitchen. Mom was already there, and from the look of things, she'd been busy.

"Do you expect me to eat . . . all of this?" I stared at the kitchen table, which was practically buckling under the weight of all the food. Pancakes, bacon, eggs, a fruit bowl, an entire loaf of toast, and . . .

"Is that actual gruel?" I asked, pointing to a pot.

"Grits," Mom answered, wiping her hands on a dish towel stuck in her waistband. "And no," she continued, "you don't have to eat all of it. I just . . . I want you to start your day off right."

I grabbed a plate and some bacon. "Mom, you didn't make this much food the day Finn and I chased our first werewolf. I'm pretty sure today will be less challenging than that." I was trying to joke, but Mom frowned.

"I don't think I ever made you girls any food. Finn could make mac and cheese by the time she was four, and you were using a microwave by that age. I should've cooked more."

I stared at her. "Mom, we were fine. And I happen to like SpaghettiOs. Especially the kind with the meatballs. Finn used to give me the meatballs out of her bowl, and—"

I hate crying. The tears, the snot, the red face. All of it. But what I really hate is when crying sneaks up on you unexpectedly. So I looked down at my plate and shoved a piece of bacon into my mouth, hoping that would stop the sob that was welling up in my throat.

You need these meatballs more than I do, Junior. You're so skinny, a shifter is gonna pick his teeth with you one day.

Mom had turned back to the sink. "Hurry up before you miss your bus," she said, and I could've imagined it, but her voice sounded a little watery, too.

The bacon might as well have been made of cardboard for as much as I tasted it, but I got it down. "Right. Okay. Well. I, uh, guess I'll go wait for the bus."

Mom turned. "Do you want me to wait with you?"

I did. A lot. Why was hunting monsters *less scary* than waiting by a freaking stop sign in the suburbs? But I shrugged. "No, don't worry about it. I think I can handle standing on a corner by myself for ten minutes."

The parentheses deepened around her mouth. "Don't get smart."

"I wasn't! I . . ." Sighing, I shouldered my backpack. It was the same one I used to take when Finn and I would patrol, but this time there were no crossbows or vials of holy water. Just notebooks and two packs of pens.

"I'll be home after three," I told Mom.

"Okay," she replied. "Remember, main thing today is just to start getting yourself situated. Head down—"

"Eyes open," I finished for her. That might as well have been the Brannick family motto.

Mom gave a sharp nod. "Right. We'll talk when you get home. And . . ."

She walked over and, to my surprise, gave me a hug. "Have a good day, Iz."

I hugged her back, closing my eyes and breathing in the safe, familiar smell of Mom. Brannicks aren't huggers, and I couldn't remember the last time Mom had wrapped her arms around me. "I will."

The kitchen was right off the main hallway leading to the front door. The old owners of the house had put up a little shelf with hooks, a box for keys, and a tiny mirror to, I don't know, check your lipstick before you went out or whatever. I snagged my black jacket from one of the hooks, and as I did, caught a flash of movement.

Torin.

In the mirror, he leaned against the wall behind me. "Nervous?" he asked, grinning.

Glancing down the hall toward the kitchen, I leaned in closer and whispered, "No."

His grin got bigger. "Yes, you are. You're a Brannick, a Queen Among Women, and you're scared of going to school. When, really, it's the school that should be scared of you."

He said it like that was something to be proud of. Mom was still banging pans, water running in the sink, but I kept my voice as low as I could. "What the heck does that mean?"

"Like I said," Torin replied, "you're a Brannick. Not only have you been trained to dispose of the most powerful creatures this world has ever known, you've been bred to be an effective killer. Over one thousand years of genetics, all coming together to form Isolde Brannick, a deadly weapon."

I stared at him. "Torin, is . . . is this your idea of a pep talk?"

His brow wrinkled. "A what? I am simply trying to make you feel more confident about your day by giving you a small speech on your many virtues."

Adjusting my bag on my shoulder, I poked at the glass. "That's a pep talk, then. Except yours isn't really helping." Now Torin was leaning back against the wall, his arms folded over his chest. "I actually felt it was going quite well, and I hadn't even gotten to the part where I declare you a tiger sent to matriculate among kittens."

In the kitchen, the water shut off. I glared at Torin. "I'm not a *tiger*," I hissed. He gave one of his elegant shrugs as Mom called, "Iz?"

She stepped out of the kitchen, but by then, Torin had already vanished from the mirror.

"Yeah?" I replied, hoping I sounded casual.

"Just . . . be careful today, okay?"

It was such a weird thing for her to say. I mean, it was a perfectly normal thing for regular moms to say, but not for *mine*. And for a second, I wondered if I actually could be the sort of person who had a mom who told her to "be careful." The kind who rode buses and whose mom cooked breakfast.

Then she added, "Lie low. And remember your cover."

The bus ride ended up being easier than I'd thought. I snagged a seat by myself and spent the twenty-minute ride watching the boring streets of Ideal flash by and trying to tell myself that I'd faced off with werewolves and demons, for heaven's sake. Not one other kid on this bus had done that. So how tough could it be navigating high school? All I had to do was go into the main office, hand the secretary my (fake) paperwork, get a schedule, and then . . . go to class. Mom and I had agreed I shouldn't start asking questions about the attack on the science teacher too quickly, but I could definitely keep my ear to the ground.

I'd studied a map of the school last night, but that didn't prepare me for the crush of people and confusing warren of hallways and stairs and classrooms as I walked through the giant double doors. It was so . . . *loud*. To my left, a group of girls shrieked and laughed about something, while just in front of me, two boys were shouting at each other, earbuds jammed firmly in their ears.

Pushing my shoulders back, I tried to move with the same sense of purpose that everyone else seemed to have, but that wasn't really helpful since I didn't actually know where I was going. I wandered down one hallway, only to have to double back when it dead-ended in a row of lockers. Then I thought I'd found the main office, but that was actually the attendance office.

"The main office is in the east wing," the harried attendance lady had told me, and I'd nodded and mumbled, "Thanks," like I knew where the heck the east wing was.

Well, other than east, obviously.

By the time I found the main office, it was nearly time for first period, and the secretary hardly looked at my papers. "Here," she said, shoving a folder at me. "Schedule and list of extracurricular activities. Now get moving before third bell."

Third bell? There hadn't even been one so far.

At that moment, a harsh buzzing filled the air, and as I stepped out into the corridor, kids suddenly began to sprint for the staircases and other hallways. Pressing myself against the wall, I struggled to open the folder and not get run over. As I did, I kept up a running monologue with myself. *Oh my God, chill out. Your heart is going a million miles an hour over a bunch of kids? You fight monsters. Get a hold of yourself, Brannick.*

And I'd almost managed to do that when a boy nearly a foot taller than me collided with my shoulder, sending the folder spinning out of my hands, papers scattering everywhere.

My muscles tensed, and before I could stop it, my

hand had darted out to . . . I don't know, grab the guy, or punch him, or who knew what. Thank God he'd already moved too far past me, and my hand just flopped harmlessly in midair.

Taking a deep breath, I tried to calm down. The last thing I needed was to let my instincts take over before I'd even set foot in my first class. I knelt down and started to pick up my papers.

"Hey, you okay?"

A boy about my age stood in front of me. Sandy brown hair fell in his eyes, which, I noticed, were dark brown. "Just, uh, dropped some stuff."

Crouching down, the boy gathered up my schedule and list of school clubs while I fished the map out from under the water fountain. "You must be new," he said, and my head shot up.

"How did you know?"

"Um, the folder saying 'NEW STUDENT' kind of gave it away."

Oh, right. Now that he mentioned it, that was scrawled across the top. "Ah," I said, unsure of what else to say.

"And according to this," he continued, brandishing my schedule, "you and I have first period English together. Come on, I'll walk you."

As I followed him, the boy adjusted his dark green

backpack covered in various badges that read things like, "Rusted Nail," and "The Filthy Monkeys." I figured either those were bands, or this kid was in the weirdest Boy Scout troop ever.

"I'm Adam," he threw over his shoulder. When I just nodded, he stopped. "I'm assuming you have a name, too."

"Oh. Yeah. Izzy. My name is Izzy."

Adam inclined his head. "Well, nice to meet you, Izzy."

There was another bell, the second one, and I heard doors begin to close. "Is that—" I started, but Adam waved a hand. "You're new and I was showing you around and being a good citizen. We're good. So." Still walking, he held up the list of extracurricular activities. "Have you picked which of our fine organizations to join yet?"

I took the paper back. "Seeing as how I've been here all of five minutes, no. And besides, I'm not much of a joiner."

"Fair enough," he said amiably, leading me up a staircase. "But hey, at least you know if you get a sudden urge to be part of a chess club, or a lacrosse team, or a ghost-hunting society, you'll have the option."

I froze on the fifth step. "A what?"

Adam turned, shoving a handful of hair out of

his eyes. "Lacrosse? It's this sport with sticks, and—"

"Not that," I said, scanning the list. "Do you have a ghost-hunting group?" And sure enough, there it was on the list, the Paranormal Management Society. Trying to hide my glee, I folded the paper up and shoved it into my back pocket with a nonchalant shrug. "I mean . . . that's just weird."

Adam snorted and started climbing the stairs again. "That's one word for it. The chick that runs it, Romy Hayden, is a total wack job. Which you'll see since she's in English with us. And speaking of"—he stopped in front of a door and gave a bow—"here we are."

CHAPTER 7

By the time we walked into class, everyone was already in their desks, and I felt thirty pairs of eyes suddenly land on me.

It was not the best feeling.

"This is Izzy," Adam announced to the teacher. According to my schedule, she was Mrs. Steele, and Adam was right: she didn't seem put out by our lateness. "Welcome to Mary Evans High, Izzy," she said to me. "Why don't you take a seat near the front for today. Romy, can you move over one desk?"

I spun around, wanting to catch sight of this girl. It wasn't like I thought her little ghost-hunters club would actually be that useful. Every once in a while, groups like that spring up somewhere in the country, and they have a really bad tendency to result in a high body count.

Nothing more dangerous than civilians who think they can track Prodigium, Mom had said a few years ago after she'd had to go clean up after one of those groups. "Kids read a few books, watch a couple of stupid TV shows, and get in over their heads before they know what's happened."

But still, if I was looking for a vengeful ghost, this was a start, and a heck of a lot better one than I'd thought I'd get.

A tall Asian girl got out of one of the desks in the first row, and I realized I'd seen her on the bus. It would've been hard to miss her. Next to my all-black ensemble she was a riot of color. Her jeans were bright red, and her white T-shirt had two rainbows splashed across it, with the words DOUBLE RAINBOW ALL THE WAY written in electric-blue bubble letters. A hat that same vivid blue was yanked low on her head, and the frames of her glasses were neon purple. When got up, I noticed she was wearing red Converse sneakers.

As she sagged into the other desk, she flipped up the dark lenses of her sunglasses, revealing regular glass underneath. "Enjoy that desk. It's one of my favorites."

I didn't know what to say to that. Mom said to get close to people, find stuff out. Investigate. What she'd neglected to mention was how. Should I introduce myself to Romy now? Use the cover story? Or was that too much too soon?

Luckily, I was literally saved by the bell. It trilled, and Mrs. Steele started handing out work sheets. I spent the next fifty minutes using words like "inscrutable" in a sentence. When class ended, Romy bolted for the door, so I didn't have to practice my cover story after all.

Next up was P.E., the one class I wasn't that worried about. Mom had had me and Finn running at least six miles a day basically since we could walk. Besides, in all the TV shows Mom had gotten me, people usually just spent P.E. talking under the bleachers, or meeting up with their secret boyfriends. Since I didn't have anyone to talk to, or a boyfriend, secret or otherwise, I figured I had this.

Or I would have if I'd been able to find the gym. It took me a while to figure out that the gym was actually an entirely separate building, slightly downhill from the school itself. And once I finally got there, I realized there was one thing I didn't have: a uniform. Everyone else was coming out of the locker rooms in these awful gray shirt/shorts combos with MEHS scrawled across the chest.

The coach, a tubby guy who was about my mom's age, looked me up and down and barked, "You! Why aren't you dressed out?"

Before I could answer, a voice called, "She's new, duh."

It was Romy. Dressed all in gray, she seemed smaller than she had earlier. The coach frowned at her. "Attitude!"

"Sorry," she said, sounding anything but. Then she turned to me. "He basically shouts everything. You'll get used to it."

And then, to prove her point, the coach yelled, "Okay, you over here!" He waved at my half of the gym, "You're Team A, rest of you are Team B. Opposite sides, let's go!"

Groaning, Romy pushed her glasses up her nose.

"Teams for what?" I asked as the kids next to us began heading for the nearest wall.

"Effing dodgeball," she said with a long sigh.

Dodgeball. Right. I'd heard of that. And it seemed kind of self-explanatory. Clearly, there'd be balls. And then we'd . . . dodge.

Sure enough, the coach began placing a line of red rubber balls between our two "teams."

"I swear to God, if my glasses get broken again, I'm suing this crappy school," Romy muttered darkly under her breath. When she caught me looking at her, she added, "Twice last year. Two pairs." She raised her voice, her eyes fixed on the coach's back. "This game is barbaric!" she called.

"Zip it, Hayden," the coach replied with the air of

someone who had said those three words many, many times.

Romy scowled but stepped into line. I stepped next to her, tugging at the hem of my hoodie.

"What's your name?" Romy asked. A tiny dimple flashed in one cheek. "I mean, in my head, you'll always be The Girl Who Took My Desk, but that's kind of an awkward thing to call you all the time."

"Izzy."

"Ah, a fellow holder of a cutesy name. So you're new?"

I nodded, but before I could say anything else, the coach blew his whistle. At the sound, several kids darted forward and grabbed the rubber balls. Before the whistle had even faded, a tall boy on the other side of the gym took aim at Romy and threw.

The ball didn't hit her glasses at least, but it did slam into her forearm with a meaty smack. Romy winced, rubbing the red mark already forming on her skin. As the tall boy laughed and high-fived one of his friends, Romy called out, "Yeah, nice one, Ben. You took out a ninety-pound myopic chick. Congratulations on your masculinity!" With that, she trudged over to the bleachers.

Out of the corner of my eye, I caught a ball zooming at me, but I jerked back so that it sailed harmlessly by. Okay. I could do this. It was actually kind of similar to a training exercise Mom used to make me and Finley do. That involved dodging a much heavier ball made of leather, but the principle was the same. It was one of Mom's favorite training exercises because it combined both strength and agility. Finley had always been better than me at the strength part, but agile? That I could do.

By now, kids were getting hit all over the place, and soon there were only five of us on our side of the gym, and six on the other side. One of those was the tall boy, Ben, who had hit Romy. I guess some girls would've thought he was cute, but all I could see was "psychotic jerk who goes out of his way to hit girls."

His gaze locked with mine, and one corner of his mouth lifted in a smirk. Rearing back on one leg, like he was pitching a baseball, Ben hurled a red rubber ball directly at me. He threw it so hard that I actually staggered back a step when I caught it. But I did catch it. Ben's smirk turned into a frown, I guess because he'd been looking forward to seeing me sprawled across the gym floor.

"Too bad, buddy," I muttered under my breath. And with that, I threw the ball back at him.

I meant to hit him in the arm, the same place he'd hit Romy. I didn't mean for it to hurt—okay, so maybe I meant for it to hurt a *little* bit—but the second the ball was out of my hands I knew I'd thrown it too hard. The ball we trained with back home was made of boiled leather. It was heavy and required some real heft to get it through the air. This ball was rubber, but I'd put the same amount of force behind it.

It hit Ben's shoulder and sent him skidding across the hardwood, his sneakers shrieking as he slid. Arms pinwheeling, he stumbled back against the far wall of the gym before finally collapsing in a heap.

For a second, everything was deadly quiet. Then the coach's shrill whistle pierced the air. "You!" he barked, letting the whistle fall from his lips. "New girl! What's your name?"

I was suddenly very aware of everyone in the gym staring at me. Crap.

Straightening my shoulders, I faced the coach. "Izzy Brannick."

"Okay, Izzy Brannick, do you wanna tell me why you just knocked McCrary here on his butt?"

Confused, I glanced over at Ben. One of his friends was helping him up. His face was pale, and when the other boy touched his shoulder, Ben winced.

"I was just . . . playing the game," I replied, and this time there was a little waver in my voice.

"He was *out*," the coach said, and when I just stared at him, he shook his head. "You caught his throw. So he was already out. There was no need to throw the ball at him, and certainly no need to—" He broke off to look at Ben, and his eyes went wide. "Dear God, did you *dislocate his shoulder?*"

Ben did look a little . . . crooked.

"I didn't mean to," I said, but the coach wasn't listening. "Get him to the nurse's office," he called to the boy beside Ben. Then his gaze swung back to me. "And you. You . . . just go run some laps. Until the end of the period."

"Seriously, it was an accident—" I said, but Coach Lewis just pointed at the double doors. "FOOTBALL FIELD. LAPS."

I heard a few giggles, and Romy was squinting at me, but basically everyone else in the gym was watching me with a combination of dislike and fear. Suddenly I saw myself through their eyes—all in black, my hair scraped back from my face—and I wondered how "fitting in" had ever seemed possible.

CHAPTER 8

The football field was right behind the gym, just down the hill. In addition to the running track circling it, the field also boasted several sets of rickety-looking bleachers. I jogged down the steps to the track, my breath coming out in small white clouds. My cheeks were still so hot, I was surprised they didn't steam in the cold air.

The sun was bright overhead, and I realized with a start that it was only around nine in the morning. Not even lunch and I'd already nearly killed someone. What had Torin said about me going to a regular school? That I was a tiger and they were kittens? I didn't feel much like a tiger, and that Ben kid hadn't looked like a kitten, but still. He was the one going to the nurse's office, and I was the one being punished.

Not that this was real punishment, I guess. Running, I could do.

The track around the football field wasn't even a real track. It was more like a well-worn path, the packed dirt showing through the brown, dry grass. Glad I'd chosen sneakers instead of boots (although I was pretty quick in those, too), I set off.

The February air knifed through my lungs, every breath burning. But with each thump of my sneakers against the track, I started to feel a little more . . . okay, so "normal" probably isn't the greatest word, but less crappy at least. Mom always said that exercise was the best cure for everything. Finn and I knew a mission hadn't gone well when Mom came back to the compound and spent a few hours on the training field.

Man, what I wouldn't have given for that field now. A couple of laps around a lame high school track was one thing, but kicking the heck out of a dummy or flinging some throwing stars would've felt a lot more satisfying.

Picking up my speed, I rounded the corner, and suddenly felt like someone was watching me. I glanced up, and sure enough, there was a guy in the bleachers. I only caught a few details as I jogged past—wavy black hair, sunglasses, something weird about his jacket—and when he lifted one hand to wave at me, I ignored him.

He was still there when I went around the second time, but now he was standing up, hands shoved into his pockets, shoulders up against the cold. "Weirdo," I muttered. Okay, so maybe the girl who had just laid out a guy with a dodgeball had no room to talk, but still. Even *I* knew it wasn't socially acceptable to stare at people.

I pulled my hoodie up and kept running, faster now, and when I made the lap the third time, the bleachers were empty. Awesome. Maybe Watcher Dude had found some other girl to creep on.

Lowering my eyes back to the track, I wondered just how many laps I was supposed to do. The coach had just said "some." Was that a set number that everyone else who went to high school already knew? Did that mean I had to run until the end of P.E.? And would I even be able to hear the bell out—

Suddenly, a pair of shiny black shoes came into view directly in front of me. Watcher Dude was standing in the middle of the track. He didn't move as I darted to the side, my sneakers skidding on the dirt as I slowed down.

Breathing hard, I whirled around to face him. "The heck?" I panted.

He took off his sunglasses, and as he hooked them in the collar of his shirt, I noticed that the arms were bright aqua. His eyes were nearly the same shade of blue as he squinted at me. "Is someone trying to murder you?"

"What?"

Shrugging, he put his hands in the pockets of his jacket. The other boys I'd seen at Mary Evans High were wearing pullover fleeces or North Face jackets, like Adam. This guy was wearing a navy peacoat, and there was a gray scarf twisted into a complicated knot at his throat.

"I've just never seen anyone run that . . . determinedly," he said. "So I assumed someone must be chasing you." With an exaggerated lean, he peered down the track. "But that doesn't seem to be the case. So why were you running?"

"Coach Lewis told me to."

His eyebrows went up. "Ah. So you're being punished for something. Coach Lewis is not the most creative man when it comes to discipline. So let's see . . ."

Looking me up and down, the boy began to circle me. Okay, staring was one thing, but circling? Yeah, that was totally not cool. I moved around with him. "What are you doing?"

"You've definitely got that whole tough chick thing going on. Talking back, maybe? Shouting a four-letter word when you lost a relay race?"

"It's none of your business," I snapped, even as I glanced down and realized he was wearing pin-striped pants. I didn't even know those still existed. "Why aren't *you* in P.E.?"

He finally stopped circling and reached into the pocket of his coat. Pulling out an inhaler, he waggled it at me. "Asthma. But rather than just give me another elective, the fascists who run this school make me come to P.E. every day and sit out."

"So why don't you sit out in the gym?"

Grinning, the boy slid the inhaler back into his pocket. "I figured if all I was going to do was sit there, I could at least offer commentary on the athletic prowess of my classmates. Coach Lewis, sadly, did not agree. So now I'm banished to the wilds of the football field. Much like *you*."

He slid his sunglasses back on. "And now you know my deep dark secret, so it seems only fair that you share yours with me. Oh, I'm Dex, by the way," he added. "Just in case you feel weird sharing deep dark secrets with strangers."

Maybe it was his grin, which was a nice change from the glares/looks of horror I'd gotten in the gym, but I found myself giving a little smile in return. "Izzy. And there, uh, was a dodgeball incident."

"Perhaps the most intriguing phrase I've heard uttered in some time," Dex said, rocking back on his heels. "I'm obviously going to need you to elaborate."

"This jackass hit a girl too hard with one of the balls. So I . . . hit him back."

Dex ducked his head, regarding me over the top of his sunglasses. "Aaaand?"

"And maybe I threw it a little too hard and . . . dislocated his shoulder."

"Whoa, for real?" Dex asked, and for just a second, the act—or whatever it was—slipped, and he just seemed like a normal teenage boy.

A normal teenage boy wearing a cravat, but whatever.

"It was an accident," I said hurriedly, but Dex shook his head.

"Which girl and which jackass?"

"Romy Hayden and Ben . . . something. I don't remember."

"You knocked out Ben McCrary?" he asked, eyes wide.

"It was an accident," I said again. "I threw the ball harder than I meant to."

Dex burst into laughter. "Oh my God, that is the greatest thing I've heard all week. You are my new hero."

Squinting at me, he leaned in and said, "Seriously, I might actually be in love with you now. Would it be awkward if we made out?"

Head spinning, I stepped back. I thought of my cousin, Sophie, and her boyfriend, Archer. The way they were always zinging one-liners back and forth. I should have a one-liner. Instead, I said, "Yes, it would be."

I waited for his smile to falter, for a little bit of that light to fade from his eyes. But if anything, he looked *more* delighted. "Well, then we'll just have to hold off until we know each other better."

Wait, did that mean he actually *wanted to make out with me*?

"And not only did you assault Ben McCrary—"

"I didn't *assault* him," I muttered, but Dex ignored that.

"You did it in defense of Romy Hayden, who is one of the least useless people at this school. I'm not joking. You are my favorite person today."

From somewhere in the distance, I heard the electronic whine of the bell, and Dex frowned. "Sadly, our time together has come to an end. Unless you have Algebra Two next?"

I shook my head, thinking back to the schedule I'd shoved into my back pocket. "European history."

"Ah, you're a sophomore. I'm a junior, so ships in the night are we," Dex said, heaving a sigh. "In that case, I'll see you on the bus tomorrow."

I blinked. "You ride my bus?"

"You didn't notice me this morning? I'm wounded."

I'd been too busy worrying about how I was going to navigate Mary Evans High to notice anyone, even a six-foot-tall boy wearing pinstripes.

"Not much of a morning person," I finally said.

Bouncing on the balls of his feet, Dex smiled again.

"Fair enough. I'll save you a seat tomorrow. Until then, Isabella."

"Isolde," I corrected, and his smile widened.

"Even better." He reached out to shake my hand.

Our palms touched, and a jolt went through me. He didn't seem to feel it as he gave my hand two firm shakes before dropping it. "Try not to kill anyone else today!" he called as he began walking backward down the track.

I was still reeling, so it took everything I had to muster up a weak smile in reply. Once he'd turned around and started walking like a normal person, I glanced down at my hand.

My skin still tingled, like a low electric current was running through me. It was faint, and I'd certainly felt stronger, but it was unmistakable. Magic.

Dex was Prodigium.

CHAPTER 9

The rest of the day passed uneventfully. I guess after you've beaten someone up with a dodgeball and flirted with a monster, most anything else will seem pretty tame.

I wasn't quite ready for another run-in with Dex, so rather than take the bus home, I decided to walk. It was a few miles, and by the time I got home, my calves ached, but the walk gave me time to think. What kind of Prodigium was Dex? Warlock seemed like the most reasonable explanation—I hadn't spotted a bloodstone on him, and without one of those, vampires become barbecue in the sunlight—and there hadn't been that weird animal smell that seemed to cling to shape-shifters. Wings were pretty conspicuous, so unless he was hiding them underneath that peacoat, I didn't think he was Fae. But I'd been around lots of witches and warlocks, and I'd always been able to sense their power once I got within a few feet of them. I'd never had to *touch* one to feel their magic.

As I unlocked the front door, I tried to think of who I could ask about this. I knew I should tell Mom, but I'd never had trouble identifying a Prodigium before, and it wasn't something I was ready to own up to. Besides, this was meant to be my case. My chance to prove myself.

I wondered what Finley would say if she were here. Probably something like, "Stab him with silver and see if it kills him."

So that left me with only one option.

The house was quiet and dark when I stepped into the foyer, and Mom's car wasn't in the driveway. Still, I found myself walking softly as I made my way to the third bedroom. I hadn't been in there since we'd moved in, and when I opened the door, it was like being punched in the stomach.

Finley's things were in here. By which I meant her pillow and a photograph she'd had stuck to the mirror in our bedroom. It showed us when I was around six, Finn eight or nine. We were in the training yard, two little redheaded girls with our arms around each other's shoulders. It was a sweet picture (if you ignored the fact that I was holding a miniature crossbow and Finn's fingers were wrapped around the hilt of a sword), and

I wished I remembered the day it had been taken.

There was also her belt, the one I'd found that night, slung around one of the bedposts. I wanted to go over to it, to hold it in my hands. Instead, I walked past the bed and over to the mirror that hung on the wall. It was, as usual, covered with a heavy piece of canvas. When I pulled it back, Torin was there, hip propped against the bed behind me.

He was examining his fingernails, bored, but when he realized I was there, his face brightened. "Hullo, Isolde. Pleasant day at school?"

"Not really," I told him. "But I needed to ask you something."

Torin folded his arms. "I'm not in much of a prophecy-spouting mood today, to be honest."

"I don't need to know the future. I need to know . . . I don't know, the present, I guess. I met this boy today, and he's . . . I don't know, he's something."

"Something as in he is handsome and you fancy him, or something as in he's one of my kind?"

Scowling, I replied, "He's Prodigium. I think. I don't know He felt strange when I touched him."

The second the words were out of my mouth, I regretted them. Torin's sly grin only intensified that regret.

"This is why I told Aislinn she should have more

blokes around. A boy touches you, and you mistake hormones for magic."

I wanted to shake the frame, but I crossed my arms, mimicking his pose. "It wasn't hormones. It was magic. Or some kind of power. But not like any power I've felt before. It's . . . I don't know, really weak."

Finally, the grin slipped and Torin managed to look a little serious. "Weaker than mine?"

Even trapped in the mirror, Torin radiated power, and I nodded. "Yeah. I can usually pick up on a Prodigium within a few feet. But this guy, I didn't get it until he shook my hand. Could he just be . . . like, a really, really bad warlock?" But then I shook my head. "No, wait. He had asthma. If he were a warlock, he would've cured that." One of the benefits to being a magical being was that they almost never get sick.

Torin gave an elegant shrug. "Perhaps he's faking it. And something could be diluting his power. A counter-spell or a binding charm. Did he seem odd?"

I thought back to Dex, to his weird, formal way of talking, and strangely old-fashioned, if stylish, outfit. "Yeah, but I'm not sure that's magic."

"If you find out where he lives, I can always slip into his mirror, find out for certain," Torin offered. "It would be, as you like to say, a gigantic pain in my backside, but I could try."

Torin moved pretty easily through the mirrors in our house because his original mirror was housed here. Getting into mirrors in other locations was tough for him, but I'd seen him do it before. And I'm not going to lie: the idea of sending Torin to check up on Dex was tempting. What if Dex was something dangerous? Okay, so maybe an asthmatic guy rocking a cravat didn't seem all that threatening, but what did I know? And I was here to investigate supernatural shenanigans.

But I couldn't get over the feeling that sending my pet warlock into a dude's mirror to spy on him was . . . well, icky. Especially when he was one of the few people at school who'd been nice to me today. So I shook my head. "No, let's not go that far. I'll work it out on my own."

"As you like," Torin said, going back to studying his cuticles. "But the offer stands."

I leaned back on the bed, bracing my arms on the footboard. In the mirror, it looked like we were standing practically on top of each other. "You just want me to owe you a favor."

"There is but one favor you can do for me, Isolde, and that is to release me from this prison."

The words sent a shiver through me. "That's never going to happen."

He glanced up, raising an eyebrow. "Oh, so now it's

you with the gift of prophecy, is it? I know what I've seen. You are my key and my salvation."

Without answering, I got up and went to cover the mirror. His voice sounded muffled behind the canvas as he called, "Remember, a favor for a favor, Isolde. I can be very useful."

He could be. He *had* been. But his visions never came when we most needed them, and from everything Mom had told me, Torin had a way of twisting words and promises so that he got more than you were willing to give, and always gave you less than you wanted.

In other words, it wasn't worth it.

Sighing, I opened the door and walked into the hallway.

"What are you doing?"

I jumped as Mom's voice rang out in the quiet house. She was standing just inside the front door, frowning. "Isolde?" she asked, her body stiff.

I froze, a million lies rushing to my lips. But Mom always saw through those, and all lying did was piss her off. "I was talking to Torin."

"About what?"

"Just my day at school." That wasn't *technically* a lie, but Mom still frowned.

"Well, why don't you tell *me* about your day." Her

expression hardened. "Specifically the part where you hurt some boy in your P.E. class?"

Ugh. So that's why she was so pissed. "It was an accident," I said for what felt like the millionth time that day, but Mom gave a frustrated sigh as she tossed her bag onto the hall table. "Damn it, Izzy, I told you, keeping a low profile is an essential part of every job."

"I was trying!"

"And breaking someone's arm by second period? That was your attempt at *trying*?"

"It was only a dislocated shoulder," I muttered, sounding sullen even to my own ears. "And he was a jerk who purposely hurt this girl I think can help me with the ghost thing."

Mom gave a frustrated sigh, but then what I had said dawned. "What does that mean?"

Briefly, I told her about the Paranormal Management Society and Romy. As soon as I said the words "teenage ghost hunters," she sat down on the edge of the bed.

"Damn it. You know if there is a legitimate haunting happening here, they'll probably end up making things worse. Those types of kids always do."

"Yeah," I said, going to sit next to her. "But it's something. If nothing else, maybe they'll have information. Either about Mr. Snyder himself, or who could be haunting the school. Save me the hassle of going to the library."

Mom looked up, and something very close to a smile flickered on her face. "So you'd actually go to a library instead of plugging everything into the Google?"

Now I smiled. "Mom, it's just *Google*. And yeah, you always said books were the best for research. Even the Internet can't know everything."

"I know I said that; I'm just surprised you listened."

"I do that sometimes," I told her, and she reached out and patted my knee. Then, clearing her throat, she rose to her feet and headed for the door.

"Well, it's a start," she said, her voice slightly gruff. "Probably won't lead to much, but better than nothing. Now, come on. I don't like you spending too much time in here."

Swallowing my disappointment, I stood up, too. I had always been proud of my mom. So she'd never bake cookies, or sew a Halloween costume, but she could fight *monsters*. She was tough and smart, and maybe she didn't read bedtime stories, but she had taught me to defend myself against the things that lurked under beds.

But in that moment, I didn't want a smart, tough mother who kicked supernatural ass. I wanted to sit on the couch with her and tell her about my crappy day. And maybe about Dex, leaving out the possible magical powers part.

I wanted to tell her that I missed Finley, too.

Instead, I followed her out the door and said, "So, I . . . I guess I'll go do homework now."

"Right," Mom said with a brusque nod. "And I'll go, uh, clean up the kitchen. See you at six for dinner?"

"Sure," I said, turning to jog up the stairs.

When I was halfway up, Mom called, "Izzy?"

"Yeah?"

"I'm . . . you're doing good work," she said haltingly. "Other than the dislocated shoulder."

It wasn't exactly "Oh, Izzy, I am so proud of you, and I was wrong to ever give you such lame job."

But I'd take it.

CHAPTER 10

I sat up, confused. I was moving, and overhead, birds were chirping, and the scent of flowers was so heavy in the air, it made me feel a little light-headed. Sunlight sparkled on dark green water. When I threw up my hand to ward off the glare, I saw that once again, I was wearing a ton of rings that I had never owned.

Groaning, I sank back against silken pillows. "Why are we on a boat?"

At the other end of the little rowboat, Torin grinned at me, his long arms pulling the oars. "Thought a change of scenery might be nice."

"You know what would be nice? Not having you invade my dreams with these"—I waved my hand—"whatever this is."

"It's an outing, Isolde. And quite a nice one, too."

Much as I hated that, I couldn't argue. The sun felt good on my face, and there was something undeniably pleasant about drifting down a stream flanked with flower bushes and weeping willows. "Where is this?" I asked. "Someplace you knew?"

Torin abandoned the oars and leaned back, closing his eyes and lifting his face to the sun. "You know the answer."

"Set you free and I'll find out," I muttered.

He nodded, replying, "Even so."

"Since that's not going to happen, any other reason you decided we should row our boat merrily down the stream?"

"You were grinding your teeth as you slept. It was both annoying and concerning, so I thought an outing would do you some good."

"First off, don't watch me sleep, and secondly—"

"Oh, hush," Torin said with no real heat. "Can't you just lie back on your pillows and enjoy this lovely summer's day?"

"It's February, and I *am* lying back," I reminded him.

"In the outside world," Torin said. "But in here, it can be whatever we want."

That was a dangerous line of thought. Torin was good at this kind of thing: offering dreams and wishes and perfect days. But none of it was real, and none of it was free.

Still, it was nice to feel warm and drowsy in the sunshine, not worrying about Finley or Mom or ghosts or—*shudder*—high school.

Leaning over the side of the boat, I let my fingers trail in the cool water. It took me a second to realize I didn't have a reflection. Sitting up, I squinted at Torin. "I get the no-mirrors thing, but even water is unreflective?"

"My rules," he said easily.

There was a flash of movement on the far bank, and I lifted my head to see a woman moving along the shore. She was wearing a heavy dress of purple brocade, the sunlight picking up hints of blue in her black hair. "Who's that?"

"Hmm?" Torin turned his head, and seeing the woman, he scowled. "What is she doing here?"

A flick of his wrist, and the woman vanished; but Torin kept scowling. "That's odd. I didn't invite Rowena here." He squinted at me. "Did you?"

"Since I don't even know who Rowena is, no."

Torin turned his gaze back to the spot where she'd been. "Rowena was a member—" He broke off, brushing his hair out of his eyes. "No matter."

I sat there waiting for him to say more, but Torin simply closed his eyes, tilting his face to the sun. I didn't know much about the life he'd lived pre-mirror, and sometimes I wondered if that was for the best. It was too weird to think of Torin as just a normal guy—a normal *boy*, really—wandering around in the world.

We were quiet for a long time, and I might have dozed off. Was that even possible? Sleeping inside of a dream? With Torin, who knew? Still, I was startled when he suddenly said, "You should just be yourself."

"What?"

"You're afraid these children won't like you. That's what you were grinding your teeth over in your sleep. Worrying how to make them like you, how to infiltrate their little group."

He lifted his head, looking at me intently. "But the person you are is delightful, and they will like you if you'll just . . . be that."

I shifted, smoothing imaginary wrinkles in my heavy skirt. "So that's your big advice? Be myself?"

Torin grinned, his teeth slightly crooked, but very white. "That's it. Be yourself. Be Isolde Brannick, and they will have no choice but to adore you." He reached out and took my hand, pressing a kiss to the back of it.

I was too stunned to do anything but sit there, my hand limp in his.

When Torin lifted his head, his eyes were bright green, almost the same green as the water we floated on. "Now, wake up," he whispered.

I came awake almost instantly, my stomach in knots.

According to my clock, I had three minutes before my alarm went off, pale gray light shining around the edges of my curtains.

Immediately, my eyes shot to the mirror, but there was no trace of Torin there. Which, considering how weirded out I felt, was a good thing. What the heck had that been? The hand-holding in the last dream had been one thing, but hand-kissing was, to quote Maya, a whole 'nother ball of wax.

Still unsettled, I threw back my covers and headed downstairs.

Mom had already left. This time, there was no huge breakfast spread. Just a Post-it on the freezer reminding me that there were frozen waffles inside. I popped a couple into the toaster, then went back upstairs and took the hottest shower I could stand. As I stood under the spray of scalding water, I thought about my dream last night. Not the hand-kissing stuff—I definitely didn't want to think about that—but the stuff that came before.

Be yourself, Torin had said. I could do that. And hey, so maybe yesterday was less than ideal—ha! pun alert—but I had at least made friends with Romy. Kind of. So now all I had to do was talk to her about the ghost hunter club and see if she knew anything about the attack on that science teacher.

Easy.

I felt better when I got out of the shower, but I also discovered that my little inner pep talk had taken longer than I thought. My waffles were burned *and* I was in danger of missing the bus.

Throwing on some clothes—jeans, another black T-shirt, and, remembering the looks I got yesterday, the one pink hoodie I owned—I ran out the door. The stop was down the block, and the bus doors were starting to close as I rushed up. My hair was still damp on my shoulders as I hoisted myself up the steps, giving what I hoped was an apologetic smile.

The driver—Maggie, according to her name tag—gave a disdainful sniff. "I don't wait," she snapped at me. "You lucked out this time, girlie."

"Sorry," I mumbled, making my way to the back. I scanned the rows for an empty spot, and suddenly Dex stood up, waving his arms. "Isolde!" he called. "It's me, Dex, your new best friend! I saved you a seat!"

Several of the kids around him turned to glare, but Dex either didn't notice or didn't care. I lifted my hand, acknowledging him. He sat there beaming at me, looking as threatening as a golden retriever, but I couldn't forget what happened yesterday. If I knew Dex was Prodigium, did he know what I was? Is that why he was so buddy-buddy this morning?

The bus lurched forward just as I got to the back, and Dex reached out to steady me. I think he was trying to grab my waist, but his hand landed on my hip. Even through my jeans I felt that low hum of magic.

Dex jerked back, and for a second I thought maybe he'd felt it too. But then he winced and said, "Sorry. We probably haven't reached the inappropriate touching stage of our friendship yet."

Oh, right. I'd been so concerned with trying to figure out what Dex *was* that it didn't even occur to me that a boy had just touched my hip, which was definitely in the "bathing suit zone." That was as far as Mom had gotten in her Facts Of Life talk a few years back: "Don't let boys touch you in the bathing suit zone." Then the warlock she and Finn had been chasing chose that moment to leap onto the hood of our car, and the rest of her talk had gone unfinished.

I think Mom had been relieved.

Blushing, I sat down next to Dex, trying to keep our thighs from touching. (Thighs were not in the bathing suit zone, but I was pretty sure they were still kind of scandalous.)

As I reached behind me to start braiding my hair, Dex propped his ankle on the opposite knee. Today he was wearing gray corduroys and a deep navy V-neck that made his eyes look even bluer. The peacoat was balled up behind his head.

I nodded at it. "Were you napping?"

"Yeah. Bus gets to my neighborhood at six thirty, which is just inhumane, if you ask me. I usually sleep the whole way, but I'll endeavor to be an alert seatmate for you."

Securing a rubber band around the end of my braid, I looked at him. "Do you always talk like that?"

"Like what?"

I raised both eyebrows. "'Endeavor to be an alert seatmate'? Who says stuff like that?"

Chuckling, Dex elbowed me in the ribs. "Civilized people. People with names like Dexter and Isolde."

"Izzy," I told him. "Only my mom calls me Isolde, and even then, just when she's mad at me." I didn't mention that Mom had been calling me that a lot lately.

"So how did you end up in Ideal, Mississippi, Izzy?" Dex asked, sitting up. His hair was tangled in the back, and I had this completely bizarre urge to smooth it out. Just in case my fingers decided to do that, I clasped them together, laying my hands in my lap.

"We lived in Tennessee, but then my mom, um, lost her job. So she thought a change of scenery would be good for us." There it was, my first time using the cover story. Dex accepted it with an easy shrug.

"I'm new, too," he said. "Well, newish. I moved here back in the summer."

"From where?"

Dex linked his fingers and stretched his arms over his head. "New York."

"Did your parents want a change of scenery, too?"

"They're, uh . . . not around anymore."

Surprised, I twisted to face him. "Who do you live with?"

Dex widened his eyes in mock innocence. "Oh, I live by myself. Didn't I mention? I'm thirty-five."

When I just rolled my eyes, he relented. "I live with my Nana."

He said it lightly, but Mom had taught me and Finn to pay attention to body language. Dex was twisting the strap of his bag around his fingers so tightly that his knuckles were turning white.

Before I could ask anything else, a face suddenly popped up over the seat in front of me. "Hey," Romy said. "Izzy, right?"

"That's me," I said. "Have you, um, been there the whole time?"

"Romy's like me," Dex said, nudging the back of her seat with one pointy-toed boot. "Picked up entirely too early, sleeps the whole ride."

"Tries to sleep," she corrected. "This idiot usually keeps me awake." Despite the insult, there was affection in her voice, and Dex was grinning at her.

"Anyway, just wanted to say thanks for tearing Ben McCrary's arm off yesterday."

"I dislocated his shoulder," I said, but Dex waved me off.

"I like Romy's version better. And just wait, by spring break, the story will be that you tore off *both* his arms and shattered his spine."

Romy snorted. "Did you tell her about the meeting?" she asked Dex.

"No, I was boring her with my life history first," Dex replied. "Why don't you give her the hard sell?"

Eyes twinkling behind her glasses, Romy rested her chin on her hands. "Well, since you're such a rad chick and all, we thought you might want to join our club."

I hoped my face looked confused rather than relieved. All that worrying over how I was going to get into the club, and then, *bam*, I'm invited. Maybe today really *would* be better than yesterday.

Doing my best to furrow my brow, I looked back and forth between them. There was something unnerving about their identical expressions of glee. "Um, is this one of those clubs where the first rule is you don't talk about it?"

Dexter threw his head back and laughed, and Romy made that snorting noise again. "No," she said. "But if it were, I'd definitely want you in that one, too. This is actually a school-sanctioned thing, so it counts for extra-curricular stuff on college applications."

Oh, right. College. That was something I'd have to pretend to be thinking about, too.

But then Dex sat up and said, "Romy, I don't think Harvard is going to very impressed by your membership in something called PMS."

A startled giggle burst out of me. Paranormal Management Society. PMS. I hadn't even thought of it like that.

Romy looked a little chagrined. "I didn't come up with the name, and by the time we got it, Anderson had already made the T-shirts," she insisted, which only made Dex laugh harder.

"So what is PMS?" I asked, even though I already knew. "I mean, I know the traditional definition. . . ."

"Paranormal Management Society," Romy answered, swatting at Dex.

"Oh," I said weakly. "That's . . . um . . . that's awesome."

"Okay, see, I feel like when you're saying 'awesome,' what you mean is 'lame' and 'making me not want to be friends with you,'" Dex said.

"No." I shook my head. "That doesn't sound lame at all. It's just . . . I never heard of a school-sponsored monster-hunting club. What do you guys do?"

"Mostly we lurk around places at night with dorky

equipment purchased off the Internet," Dex offered, making Romy smack his arm again.

"We research local ghost legends, and then we . . . investigate them."

Dex leaned over and said in a stage whisper, "'Investigate' is code for lurking around places at night with dorky equipment purchased off the Internet."

"We're working on doing more," Romy said quickly. "Anderson—you'll meet him later—is our resident ghost-lore researcher, and he's looking into ways we can actually, like, banish ghosts and exorcise places."

She sounded so excited, and it was all I could do not to wince. Humans getting involved with the supernatural was bad enough, but exorcisms were way more than a bunch of teenagers could handle.

"Have you guys ever found anything?" I asked.

"We thought we got some ghostly voices on a tape recorder once," Romy offered. "At this creepy abandoned house in the next town over. And Anderson's closet door opened on its own one time."

"Because he had his window open," Dex muttered, and Romy shot him a look. "*Maybe* it was because of that. We don't know. It could've been . . . other stuff."

"Sure, why not? I just, uh, don't want to wear a T-shirt that says PMS, okay?" I added, and Romy stuck out her hand. "Deal."

CHAPTER 11

We shook on it just as the bus pulled up to the school. "Try to get kicked out of P.E. again today," Dex told me as he gathered up his stuff. "We can hang on the football field."

"Ha-ha," I muttered, slinging my bag over my shoulder.

Romy and I made our way to English while Dex sauntered off to his first class. We got to Mrs. Steele's room before the second bell, so Romy tossed her backpack onto the desk next to mine and said, "Gonna run to the bathroom. Watch my bag?"

"Sure," I replied as she dashed out the door.

As soon as she was gone, my eyes fell on her bag. Should I look through it really quickly? I wasn't sure if there was anything related to PMS or the case in there, but Mom said to check everything. If anyone asked what I was doing, I could just say I was looking for a pen.

My fingers were already reaching for the strap when something heavy landed on my desk. Startled, I looked up to see Adam sitting there.

"Hi," he said, smiling.

I drew back my hand. "Um. Hi."

"So I guess you decided to be a ghost hunter after all." He was still smiling, but there was something weird in his face. He looked kind of . . . bummed.

When I didn't say anything, he hurried on. "I mean, I just saw you talking to Romy and Dexter when you walked in, and you guys seemed really friendly. Especially you and Dex."

I was so confused that all I could do was stare at him while my brain raced for something to say. Why did Adam care who I was hanging out with? "They're nice," I finally said lamely, and Adam gave a little shrug.

"So, anyway, I was going to ask you this yesterday, but . . . you know."

Adam had gone kind of red and stammery, and I braced myself for whatever it was he wanted to ask me. "Anyway," he said again, "could I get your number?"

I blinked. What—oh, my cell phone number. Which he wanted. So he could call me.

"Sure," I said, hoping I sounded normal. Because

this was normal. Boys asking for your phone number. I scrawled it across a sheet of notebook paper and handed it to him. Adam grinned, looking relieved.

"Awesome," he said, nodding his head.

Romy returned, flopping into her desk with a huge sigh. When she noticed Adam, she gave a little wave. "Hey, Lipinski."

"Romy," Adam replied, but he didn't really look at her. To me, he said, "Okay, well, I'll, uh, see you around, Izzy." He waved the piece of paper. "And call you."

"Right," I said, still wondering what his deal was.

Once he was back at his own desk, Romy leaned over. "How do you have two dudes crushing on you in less than twenty-four hours at this school?"

I whirled around. "What?"

"Lipinski practically left a drool marks on your desk, and Dex is even goofier than normal in your presence."

The third bell rang then, saving me from answering. But as I pulled out a pen and paper for Mrs. Steele's vocabulary quiz, I snuck a glance at Adam a few rows over. He was sneaking a glance at *me*, so I quickly looked back to the front of the room. There had been something kind of . . . dreamy in his expression, but that wasn't because he liked me. How could he? We'd spent all of five minutes together yesterday.

As for Dex, well, he was Prodigium. And probably

only interested in me because of that. And Adam had asked for my number because . . . actually, I couldn't think of any other reason besides that he wanted to call me. And why do boys ever call girls if not to ask them out?

Scribbling out the definition of "moratorium," I tried very hard to ignore the sinking sensation in my stomach. All that TV I'd watched aside, I really didn't know anything about normal teenage interaction. I'd prepared myself for ghosts and keeping my cover story consistent, but the one variable I hadn't even considered was . . . humans. Regular people. With regular emotions and thoughts and wants that weren't all tied up in the supernatural.

I couldn't get suspicious over every single person who showed the slightest bit of interest in me. Clearly, I was going to have to brush up on my Normal People Skills.

Maybe a new season of *Ivy Springs* was already out on DVD. . . .

By the time English ended, I'd made myself a list of things I needed to get. More DVDs, obviously, but I also wanted some of those magazines I'd seen in drugstores and gas stations. The ones with glossy-haired girls on the cover and titles like *American Teen* and *Sassy Miss*. I wanted to be both of those things. Okay, so maybe I could do without being "sassy" for now, but there had to be good info on regular teenage stuff in there. Those magazines always had articles about "How to Tell if a

Boy Likes You!" and "Could Your Lipstick Kill You?"

I'd also added "makeup?" only to cross it out. Maybe I should read that article about killer lipstick first.

Making the list cleared my head a little bit, and I was actually in a good mood once we got to P.E., despite the fact that Coach Lewis handed me a uniform as soon as I walked in. Once I was changed into the ugliest T-shirt/shorts combo on earth, I followed Romy out of the locker room and into the gym.

Ben was there, sitting on the bleachers, his arm in a sling. I waited for him to shoot me the Death Glare, but he was too busy talking to a blond girl next to him.

"Who's that?" I asked Romy, nodding toward the girl. I hadn't noticed her yesterday.

Romy heaved a sigh. "Beth Tanner, Ben's girlfriend since, like, the womb. They've been on and off for a while."

"Right now they seem . . . off," I said, which was kind of an understatement. Beth's face was the same bright red as the free-throw line, and I thought I could see tears shimmering in her eyes. Ben reached out with his uninjured arm to take her hand, but she threw it off. "Seriously, what is wrong with you?" she screamed, her voice echoing in the gym.

Now Ben was raising his voice, too. "It *wasn't me*." He lifted his injured arm as far as it would go, thanks to the sling. "How could I have done it with *this*?" As he said it, his eyes fell on me, and I swear his face paled a little.

"Dude, Ben McCrary is so terrified of you," Romy whispered, and I frowned.

Beth was shaking her head, and I realized Ben wasn't the only one who was afraid; Beth's red face and shrill voice weren't just from anger. Her movements jerky, she turned to the bleachers and picked up her bag, rifling through it. "I know you were upset, but this?"

She whipped something out of her backpack, and I felt my muscles tense up, but Beth wasn't brandishing anything like a weapon at Ben. It was a doll. The Barbie's hair was the same bright gold as Beth's, and it was even wearing a little cheerleading uniform in green and white, which, from all the bunting and banners covering the gym, I knew were the school colors.

But even from this distance I could see that there was something wrong with the doll. Its plastic limbs looked twisted and mangled, and there was a bright splash of red over its stomach. "This is sick!" Beth shrieked, shaking the doll, and Ben seemed to go even paler.

"Beth, I swear to God, I didn't hang that thing up in your locker." Once again, Ben gestured to his arm. "There's no way—"

"Liar!" she screamed, the word bouncing around the gym. That was apparently enough for Coach Lewis. He

94

turned around and blew his whistle. "Laps, all of you!"

"In here or out on the football field?" a girl asked. By this point, Beth was crying too hard to talk, and she was turning kind of purple. The coach was a similar shade, and seemed completely flustered. "I don't care!" he snapped at the girl. "Just . . . go run."

I turned to Romy, only to find her staring at Ben and Beth with a strange expression on her face. "Romy?" I asked. Half the class had already starting jogging lazily around the gym, while the other half was heading for the doors.

Grabbing my sleeve, Romy tugged me toward the second group. "We need to talk to Dex."

"About?"

But she didn't answer me.

Dex was on the bleachers again, huddled over a book. When he saw us, he waved and hopped down the steps.

"Did everyone get kicked out today? Was there a riot? Did you gang up to tear Ben McCrary limb from limb? Izzy led the charge, didn't she?"

"Shut up," Romy said, clearly thinking about something. In deference to Dex's asthma we walked around the track instead of running, while Romy filled Dex in on Beth's meltdown.

"Ah, high school romance. I never get tired of it," Dex said when she was finished.

"I think this is more than that," Romy said, chewing on a thumbnail. "What if the doll is like the frog?"

Dex stopped walking, shoving his hands into his coat pockets. "Okaaaay," he said slowly. "That's a . . . a point."

"What does any of that mean?" I asked. It was entirely too cold to be out there in a short-sleeve T-shirt and shorts, and I wished I'd brought my hoodie.

Seeing me shivering, Dex whipped off his coat and placed it around my shoulders. As he did, I caught a flash of silver on his wrist. At first I thought it was a watch, but it was actually some kind of bracelet. I was so busy trying to look for a bloodstone—I was pretty sure Dex wasn't a vamp, but it never hurt to check—that I nearly missed Romy answering me until I heard her say, "—like Mr. Snyder."

My head shot up. "What?"

"Mr. Snyder," Dex repeated. "Our current town scandal and PMS's ongoing case."

I took a deep breath, not sure how to proceed. I had to seem interested, but not *too* interested. "What happened?" I asked, figuring that was a safe question.

"He was nearly murdered by some sort of invisible being wielding a microscope," Romy answered.

"I'm going to need that explained to me," I said, and Dex mimed holding something over his head and bringing it down with force, making a sound like *Ka-DONK*.

I blew on my hands to warm them, smiling a little. "No, I understand how you can kill someone with lab equipment. It's the invisible part I'm not getting."

"Mr. Snyder was alone in that room," Romy said. "It was locked from the inside, and there aren't any windows in the lab."

That all lined up with what the newspaper article had said, although it had left out the microscope part.

"And what does the Beth doll have to do with any of that?" I asked. "And what frog?"

"About a week before Mr. Snyder nearly bit it, someone took one of the dead frogs he used in class for dissection," Dex answered, turning so that he was walking backward. "It was stuck to his door with its wee froggy head all bashed in."

I'd seen a lot of gross stuff in my day, but I still wrinkled my nose. "Ew."

"Indeed," Romy said with a shudder. "Poor frog."

"It was already dead," Dex reminded her, but Romy wasn't looking at him.

"And now the doll," she murmured under her breath.

Dex looked over the top of his sunglasses at Romy. "Sometimes I think you forget we can't all see directly into your brain, Romy. You're not exactly clarifying the situation for Izzy here."

Romy tucked her hair behind her ears. "Okay, so the police think that whoever attacked Mr. Snyder had some kind of personal grudge against him."

"Brilliant deduction on their part," Dex interjected, but Romy ignored him. "And the frog was meant as a kind of warning, some way of freaking him out. But, like we said, he was alone in the room. He swore up and down that there was no one in there and the microscope seemed to attack him on its own. Which obviously made us think *ghost*."

"It made *you* think ghost, Rome," Dex said, and Romy pushed her glasses up her nose.

"Can you think of a better explanation for a man being attacked in a locked room by something he couldn't see?"

When neither Dex nor I answered, Romy gave a brisk nod. "Exactly. And everyone knows that this place has a ghost: Mary Evans. She was the daughter of Ideal's mayor way back in the early 1900s. She actually went to this school."

"Was it called Mary Evans High then?" Dex asked. "Because that is an astonishing coincidence."

Romy was walking faster now, and both Dex and I sped up, too, Dex still walking backward. "No, back then it was named after some Confederate general. Anyway, Mary fell in love with one of her teachers."

"Gross," Dex and I said at the same time.

Ignoring us, Romy continued. "So they had this big secret romance going on for a while, and then she got knocked up."

"Double super gross," Dex said, turning on his heel so that he wasn't facing us anymore.

"So they were going to run away together," Romy said with a shrug. "Or at least that's what the teacher promised Mary. He was supposed to meet her in a cave right outside of town. It was where they'd been hooking up, apparently."

"But he lied, and then she froze to death waiting for him, and now her ghost haunts the school where she met him," I finished, almost without thinking.

It took me a second to realize that Romy and Dex had stopped walking. I stopped and glanced over my shoulder.

"How did you know that?" Romy asked. "You've lived here, what, a week?"

It had been less than that, but that wasn't how I knew this particular ghost story. There were versions of it all over the place. It didn't mean the story wasn't necessarily *true*; it was just . . . kind of boring.

I wasn't sure if I was disappointed or relieved. I'd told Mom this would be an easy case, but I hadn't expected it to be quite *this* easy. This had to be the ghost we were dealing with.

I realized Dex and Romy were staring at me, waiting for an answer. "Oh, right. The Mary Evans thing. It was, uh, in the brochure they gave my mom about the school."

Dex frowned. "We have a brochure? And it mentions the local ghost story?"

"Do you still have it?" Romy asked. "It would be a good thing to add to my file on Mary Evans."

"I think we threw it out," I said quickly, before trying to change the subject. "So you think that the ghost of Mary Evans is pissed at teachers or—"

Romy chewed her lower lip. "That's what we thought at first. But if the Barbie is a warning for Beth like the frog was a warning for Mr. Snyder, what does that—"

Suddenly, Dex stopped, pressing a hand against his chest. He made a kind of wheezing sound, and at first I thought he was joking. But then Romy grabbed his arm. "Dex?"

He fumbled in his pocket, getting out his inhaler. He took two deep pulls on it, and the wheeze slowly started to fade. One more pull and his breathing sounded normal, if kind of fast. "Sorry," he said. "Wasn't trying to be a drama queen."

"You shouldn't have been running," Romy chastised him, and he rolled his eyes.

"I was just walking quickly. And I'm fine now." He

raised his head, and while his face was a little pale, he didn't seem to be in danger of keeling over. "Anyway, why don't you go inform Anderson of this little *aha* moment? I think he has yearbook this period."

When Romy hesitated, Dex waved her on. "Don't worry. If Coach Lewis decides to grace us with his presence, I'll tell him you went to the ladies' room. That ought to scare him to death."

"You're sick, Dex," Romy told him.

"Which is why you like me. Now go."

Once Romy had dashed off, Dex turned to me. "Alone at last. So how's your second day stacking up against your first?"

"They've both been full of peril, but since today involved less maiming, I'm gonna give it the edge."

Dex laughed, but he still sounded out of breath. "I'm glad you decided to join our little ghost-busting gang."

Shrugging out of his jacket, I handed it back to him and tried to sound casual as I asked, "Yeah, what's with that? You don't strike me as the ghost-busting type."

Dex gave me a little half-smile, taking his coat. "I'm just full of mysteries, Miss Brannick," he said. "And now, if you'll excuse me, I think I'm going to head back to my bleachers and my book. But I'll see you on the bus."

I watched his retreating back, wondering just what Dex's mysteries might be.

CHAPTER 12

I'd hoped to get right to my first meeting of the Paranormal Management Society, but on the way home that afternoon, Romy informed me that for "budgetary reasons," they could only meet every other week, which meant there wouldn't be another meeting until the next Thursday. That gave me nearly ten days to wait, which was a lot longer than I'd wanted—the sooner I got this case over with, the better—but in the end, I was kind of grateful for the time.

For one thing, school was tougher than I'd expected. English was good. We were reading *Macbeth*, and while I'd never read Shakespeare before, any story that involved witches, ghosts, and a bunch of violence seemed right up my alley. History was also okay, and I was holding my own in chemistry, but geometry was one of the more evil foes I'd ever faced. I hadn't really thought much about balancing ghost busting with math problems, so it was nice to let the case take a backseat for a little bit.

In addition to giving me time to figure out homework, those ten days let me get closer to Romy and Dex. I still hadn't met the mysterious Anderson. He drove to school himself, and since he was a junior, we didn't have any of the same classes. But I sat with Romy and Dex on the bus every day, and by the time the first PMS meeting had rolled around, I felt like I was already one of the group. I wondered if all kids made friends this quickly, or if this was just unique to Dex and Romy.

PMS was holding its meeting in one of the portable classrooms behind the school, and when the last bell rang on Thursday afternoon, Romy and I made our way out there. "The state outlawed these like a million years ago," Romy told me as we walked into what was basically a trailer, "but a few schools keep them around for art classrooms or yearbook offices." She snorted. "You know, classes that don't really matter, according to the fine state of Mississippi."

This particular trailer wasn't being used this year. It smelled like erasers and damp carpet, but it had a big whiteboard and a few desks that weren't covered in scratched obscenities, so it met all of Romy's requirements. "We used to meet in the lunchroom, but the janitors were always rushing us." Romy turned to the whiteboard, picked up a blue dry-erase marker, and scrawled *1st point: Izzy*.

"So how long have you been running this thing?" I asked her as she wrote, *2nd point: Gym Weirdness/Beth/ Doll*.

"I tried to start a chapter back in junior high, but a couple of parents complained. Apparently, investigating the paranormal is the first step on the road to devil worship or something. But when we got to high school I was ready."

Once she'd written *3rd point: Tonight?* Romy turned to me with a broad smile. "I explained to Mr. Owens—he's our principal—that it wasn't, like, an occult thing." She raised her thumb, ticking off. "It's science. They study parapsychology at Duke, for heaven's sake. And"—she raised her index finger—"a few years back, Mary Evans High had a forensics club that studied old-timey murders. That is way more twisted than ghost hunting. And last but not least"—a third finger went up—"investigating popular ghost stories from this area increases our knowledge of local folklore and regionalism."

I sat on top of one of the desks, crossing my legs. "Wow. You really wanted to—I mean, to make this club." The door banged open, and a lanky boy, even taller than Dex, loped in. He had blond hair that fell nearly to his shoulders, and while he had a few acne scars and wasn't as handsome as Dex, he was still a pretty good-looking guy. Then his eyes landed on Romy, and his whole face seemed to light up.

"Hey, Rome," he said, his voice surprisingly deep. Then his eyes landed on me. "Oh. Hi."

I gave a little wave. "Hi."

"Anderson, this is Izzy," Romy said, and I noticed her face was kind of glowy, too. "She's gonna be in the club now, but we'll go over that when everyone gets here."

"Sounds good," he said affably, sitting on top of the desk closest to Romy.

"Everyone" turned out to be Dex. He arrived about five minutes later, sliding into the desk next to mine. "So, Izzy," he asked, turning those blue eyes on me, "suitably impressed by our headquarters?"

Romy tossed the dry-erase marker at him. "Okay, now that we're all here, I'm calling this meeting of the Paranormal Management Society to order. First point"—she gestured to the whiteboard—"is to welcome our newest member, Izzy Brannick. Izzy has only been at Mary Evans for about two weeks, but has already proven herself awesome by permanently crippling Ben McCrary."

"Whoa," Anderson said, looking at me with respect even as I said, "I just hit him with a dodgeball."

"I've had dreams about that," Anderson replied.

105

"Could you describe what happened in really precise detail?"

"Later," Romy answered for me. "We have a lot to cover today."

Reaching into her backpack, she pulled out a laptop. "Now, as you know, there have been several odd happenings around here lately. Today, Izzy and I observed something especially weird." Romy perched on the desk opposite from me, balancing the computer on her crossed legs. "Beth Tanner found a Barbie doll, dressed to look like her and seriously jacked up, hanging in her locker."

Anderson leaned forward in his desk. "Like Mr. Snyder and the frog," he said, eyes going wide.

"Possibly," Romy said, turning her computer so that we could all see it. There was a little folder on the desktop titled MARY EVANS, and Romy clicked on it. "Okay, so it's been common knowledge that Mary has haunted this place ever since she died."

"Forever condemned to high school," Dex said with a little shudder. "That would make me homicidal, too."

Romy didn't lift her eyes from the screen, but she frowned. "Why is she homicidal, though? I mean, over a hundred years, and up until a few months ago, the only ghostly activity was an occasional locker door opening, or things disappearing and showing up someplace weird." Clicking on an icon, Romy pulled up a document with

EVIDENCE typed in bold letters on the top. Several bullet points were listed below, including things like LOCKERS and CHALK.

When I asked what that meant, Romy closed the document, saying, "About ten years ago, an entire history class saw a piece of chalk float in midair for thirty seconds. But that's it."

Now I frowned. That did seem like quite a leap from floating chalk to dismembering frogs. It was really rare for a ghost to have that kind of control over its surroundings. If this was Mary Evans's doing, the sooner I got rid of her, the better.

Next to me, Anderson tapped a pencil against his braces. "If Mary left that doll for Beth, that kind of blows our whole teacher theory out of the water." He glanced over at me, cheeks reddening slightly. "We figured she went after Mr. Snyder because he was, you know, a teacher, and it was a teacher who, um . . . who, like—"

Sighing, Dex turned in his seat and propped his feet up on the desk next to him. "Got her in the family way."

As far as theories went, it wasn't a bad one, and I nodded. But Anderson was right: Why Beth now?

"Is there any connection between Beth and Mr. Snyder?" I asked, trying to look innocent. "Any reason the same thing that was after him would go after her?"

Romy pulled her knees up and stared into space.

"Nothing I can think of. Beth didn't even have biology this semester."

Silence fell over the trailer, the only sound Anderson's tapping at his teeth and the occasional car going by. Then Dex dropped his feet to the floor and proclaimed, "Look, I'm just going to say what everyone is thinking. Maybe history is repeating itself here. Maybe Beth and Mr. Snyder had a thing, like Mary and Mr. Gross Teacher."

Romy, Anderson, and I screwed up our faces at that, but I had to admit, it was a solid idea, and it did point even more to Mary Evans's being the actual culprit. And all I needed to know to make this place ghost-free was the "who."

Romy had clicked on something else now, a picture. It showed several people all dressed in clothes from the turn of the twentieth century. They were standing on a big lawn, and a few of the boys were holding tennis rackets. In the back, there was a girl with light hair and big eyes, a red circle drawn around her face. "That's Mary," Romy said, tapping the screen.

Dex leaned over my desk to get a better look, and I caught a whiff of some nice, woodsy scent. "She was pretty," he observed. "If I were her, I'd be chilling out in heaven, hitting on hot dead guys. Not hanging around here accosting chemistry teachers."

"She feels tied to this place," Anderson said, pointing his pencil at the laptop. "Until she gets some kind of justice, she's always going to hang around here."

It was very hard to bite my tongue on that, but I managed. Just like the rumors surrounding vampires, there's all kinds of wrong information about ghosts. If Mary Evans was stuck in this place, all the justice in the world wouldn't make her leave. She'd keep hanging around until someone put her to rest.

Romy shut down the computer. "So I'm thinking séance?"

My head shot up. "Wait, what?"

"We can contact Mary Evans through a séance," Anderson said. He nodded to the corner of the room, where a Ouija board, still in its box, sat on one of the desks. "See if we can talk to her, figure out if she's here. Maybe this weekend?"

Crap. I didn't know who invented Ouija boards, but whoever that guy was, he was a jerk. This place already had one dangerous spirit floating around; it didn't need something else called forth from a Ouija board.

"Are you guys sure that's the best idea? I mean, Ouija boards don't work, right?"

Anderson looked like I'd just insulted his grandmother. "Of course they *work*. I mean, we've never tried one before, but on TV—"

"On TV, EMP readers work," Dex threw in.

109

"And in reality, yours just has a lot of blinky lights."

"I've only had it for a few weeks, so we don't really know what the blinky lights do yet," Anderson replied, and Dex raised his hands in surrender.

"Boys." Romy sighed with a weariness that told me this wasn't the first time she'd stopped their squabbling. "Anderson's EMP reader is awesome and a very valuable tool for this club. And so is that Ouija board. So. As soon as I can find a free night when I don't have to babysit my brothers, we are going to get our séance on."

Dex snorted. "So we'll be doing the séance next summer, then?" To me, he added, "Romy is forever babysitting her little monsters."

He said it so easily, but most Prodigium I knew hate the term "monster." They find it offensive, and would never use it in casual conversation. Once again, I wondered just what the heck Dex was.

Sighing, he sat up and thumped his feet to the ground. "I for one cannot wait to hear the thrilling story behind why Mary Evans decided to upgrade from opening locker doors to attempted murder."

Romy ignored him and held up her hand for a high five. "So, Izzy Brannick, are you ready for your first experience with the paranormal?"

I slapped her palm, not sure whether I should laugh or cry. "As I'll ever be."

CHAPTER 13

"I don't think Everton really loves her."

"Of course he does," I told Torin around a mouthful of SpaghettiOs. "I mean, he gave up his dream of sailing across the world so that he could take her to prom. That has to mean something."

It was Friday night, and Torin and I were sitting in my room—well, I was. He was chilling in the mirror as usual, waiting for Mom to get home. When I'd come in from school, there'd been a note saying she'd be back later and I should fend for myself as far as dinner went. Hence the SpaghettiOs.

"No, I've known rogues like this Everton. He merely wants Leslie because he cannot have her. Once she succumbs to his charms, he'll tire of her."

I pointed my spoon at the screen, where Everton

and Leslie were currently locked in a pretty passionate embrace. "Think she's already succumbed."

"Bah," Torin said with a wave of his hand. "Mark my words, he'll discard her before this disk is completed."

I just shrugged, more interested in watching Everton and Leslie kiss than listening to Torin. I wondered if I'd ever have the chance to kiss someone. Didn't seem likely with all the monster hunting and family angst, but still. Kissing looked . . . nice.

"We could try that, next time I visit your dreams," Torin suddenly said, and my SpaghettiOs sloshed over the side of the bowl.

"What?"

Torin nodded toward the television. "Kissing. You've never done it, I'm quite good at it . . . seems like we should at least make an attempt."

Glaring at him, I scrubbed at the spot on my T-shirt. "I don't want to kiss you."

Raising his eyebrows, Torin leaned forward. "Do you not? Why?"

I sat my bowl on the desk, no longer interested in eating. "First of all, you're an evil warlock trapped in a mirror, and secondly, it would be . . . weird."

He shrugged. "Not unless you wanted it to be."

I had no idea what that even meant, so I just turned back to the TV. "I've known you my whole life," I told him, keeping my eyes on Everton and Leslie. "You basically used to babysit me when Mom and Finn were out on missions. So kissage is out of the question."

I expected him to tease me about that, but instead he waved it away. "Very well. Just thought I'd offer."

"Thanks but no thanks," I muttered, my face flaming. Now Everton and Leslie were arguing, but I'd missed what they were fighting about, and truth be told, I couldn't pay much attention anyway. I'd meant what I'd said about kissing Torin being weird. But then wouldn't it be weird with any boy I kissed?

I snuck a look at Torin out of the corner of my eye. Practice kissing in a dream wouldn't be like real kissing, after all. And—

No. No, no, no. That was a stupendously dumb idea. Torin was four hundred years older than me, and dangerous and trapped in a freaking mirror. My life had always been odd, but I wasn't about to let it get *that* odd.

I reached up and hit stop on the DVD player. "Okay, that's enough *Ivy Springs* for today."

Torin made a sound of protest. "But Leslie was just accusing him of fancying that other girl, Lila! And I was so sure Everton was moments away from throwing her over at last!"

"We'll watch more tomorrow," I promised him. "Now, you—"

I was interrupted by an insistent buzzing coming from somewhere in my backpack.

"What on earth is that?" Torin asked, and suddenly I remembered: my cell phone.

I scrambled to get it out of my bag. "Mom?"

There was a pause and then, "Um, no? Is this . . . is this Izzy?"

It was a boy. *What boy would be*—and then I remembered my second day of school, giving Adam this number. "Adam! Uh. Hi."

"Hi."

"Hi."

"Oh, this is scintillating," Torin muttered, and I threw him a look over my shoulder.

"So," Adam said, "I was calling because there's a basketball game tonight, and I thought you might want to, uh, come with me."

When I didn't say anything immediately, he rushed on. "I know it's really last minute, but it starts in like an hour, and we can just meet there if you want, or I can pick you up, or . . . whatever."

I glanced down at my SpaghettiO-stained T-shirt, my mind racing. A boy, coming to my house. To pick me up and take me somewhere. That was totally a date.

And I wasn't sure I was ready for that yet.

"I'll meet you there," I told him. Hopefully Mom

would be home soon, and if not, well, I could walk. After I changed into something not smeared with tomato sauce, obviously.

"Great!" he said, a little too loud.

"Yeah!" I exclaimed back, trying to match his enthusiasm. In the mirror, Torin didn't roll his eyes so much as his whole body.

"So an hour, at the school. I'll meet you there."

"Right," I agreed, hoping we could be done with this soon. My hands were starting to sweat. How come no one on *Ivy Springs* ever had these awkward phone moments? Leslie had probably never had sweaty palms in her life, not even when Everton called to tell her he was breaking up with her so that she could go to art school in Italy.

Finally Adam said, "See you then," and I breathed a silent sigh of relief. "Okay. Um . . . bye."

"Bye."

That done, I tossed my phone on the bed and turned my attention to my closet.

"Whatever shall you wear?" Torin observed, propping his chin in his hand. "Let's see, there's the black T-shirt with black jeans. Or perhaps, if you're going for elegance over function, you could wear the black T-shirt with black jeans. Ooh!" He sat up, widening his eyes. "Do you know what would be particularly fetching? The black—"

"T-shirt with black jeans," I finished for him. "Hilarious."

But looking at my closet, he did have a point. Other than that pink hoodie, my closet was a sea of sameness. A sea of black. And I didn't have the faintest idea what girls wore to basketball games.

Gripping the closet door with one hand, I leaned in and fished out a T-shirt. "You are being stupid," I muttered under my breath. "You have a ghost to hunt, and you are panicking over *clothes*."

Even though I hadn't been talking to Torin—and he knew it—he acted as though I had been. "But these things are all related, yes? The ghost and fitting in with these pathetic children. You are not fretting about clothing. You're merely trying to best maintain your cover."

Torin could be hugely annoying and a major pain in the butt, but every once in a while he said things I really needed to hear. So I threw him a very small smile before tossing a towel over my mirror.

"You know I wouldn't look," he said. "I am quite offended right now!"

Once I was in a clean shirt, I reached up to touch my hair. It was still back in the tight braid I wore every day, and for a second I thought about leaving it like that. But no, I needed to look a little different than I did at school, right?

So I unraveled the braid, combing it out with my fingers, until my hair fell in waves around my shoulders. That fixed, I grabbed a tube of lip balm out of my bag and coated my lips. I didn't own any makeup, and I knew Mom didn't have any either, so it was the best I could do.

Finally, I took the towel off the mirror to look at myself. Torin was still there, and I scowled, trying to see around him. "Lovely, Isolde," he told me, and I had to admit, I looked . . . Okay, maybe I was no Leslie, but my hair actually looked . . . pretty all down around my face like that.

Still, my hands itched to braid it again. Brannicks never wore their hair down, because it only got in the way of staking vamps or shooting shifters or taking out witches.

I heard the front door open. "Iz?" Mom called. I gave myself one last look before grabbing my jacket and heading downstairs.

Mom's hands were full of books, old ones that were flaking little bits of leather binding everywhere and filling the room with the smell of musty paper. "Everything I could get from the university library on— Oh."

She paused in the doorway. "That's a new look."

"There's this boy," I blurted out. "Adam. And he, uh, asked me to go meet him at the school for a basketball game, and I was thinking you could drive me there. If that's all right. It's part of my cover."

Mom blinked a couple of times before shifting her stack of books to her other hip. "Like a date?"

"Like a mission," I corrected, and I thought the corner of her mouth tilted up a little bit.

"Okay, then. Just let me . . . um, put this stuff away."

I walked over to help her, scooping up a few of the books. As I followed her to the guest room, I glanced at the spines. Two of them appeared to be about hauntings, but one had a title so faded I couldn't even read it. "What's the deal with all the books?" I still had no idea what Mom was up to while I was busy at school all day, although she'd mentioned driving to the university in the next town over to get some "materials."

Sighing, Mom shouldered the door open. "Research." From the tone of her voice, I knew that's all I was going to get.

Once again, a twist of guilt and anger coiled in my stomach. Did the research have something to do with Finn? If it did, I didn't understand why Mom was being so secretive about it.

"Izzy?" Mom said, and I realized she'd asked me a question.

"Sorry." I laid my books down on the bed next to Mom's half of the stack.

"I was just asking if you've found out anything at school yet."

"Yeah, actually," I told her, tucking my hair behind my ears. "For one thing, I'm pretty sure who the ghost is." I filled her in on Mary Evans and what I'd learned from PMS. When I was done, Mom raised her eyebrows. "Sounds pretty typical."

"That's what I was thinking." I perched on the edge of the bed. "Some stories become legends for a reason, I guess."

Mom nodded. "And how was the ghost hunter club? The usual?"

"Yeah. EMP detectors they ordered off of TV, files of local legends. That kind of thing. And they want to do a séance at some point, so I need to come up with a way of stopping that."

Sighing, Mom glanced down at one of her books, the one called *Ghosts and Hauntings*. "Make sure you do. Last time I dealt with one of those civilian ghost hunter groups, they did a séance. Ended up opening a portal to the Unseelie court instead, and brought through some seriously nasty faeries. I don't want to clean that up again."

I didn't know if she meant clean up in the "closing the portal, banishing the faeries" way, or if it was more a "and then I mopped the humans' blood off the wall" kind of thing.

I decided maybe it was better just to wonder.

"Anyway," I said, fiddling with the ends of my hair, "it seems pretty cut-and-dried. The frog and Barbie thing is odd, but—"

Mom held up a hand. "The what?"

Oh, right, I'd forgotten to tell Mom about Romy's theory that Mary was somehow warning her victims. As briefly as I could, I filled her in.

When I was done, Mom was frowning. "That is odd," she said. "But it doesn't really matter. If this Mary Evans is the ghost you're after, get rid of her."

"Planning on it," I told her. "But you have to do a banishing on the last day of the month, right? That's still a couple of weeks away."

Mom made a noncommittal sound in reply, and I thought of what Torin had said. Was coming here really about protecting the students of Mary Evans High? Or was it Mom's attempt at letting me have a taste of normal life?

"So this Adam," Mom said, sitting on the edge of the bed. "Is this part of the job, or is it—"

"Part of the job, for sure," I said quickly, and for some reason, Dex's face suddenly appeared in my mind. How would I feel if it were him I was meeting tonight? Just the thought sent my heart racing in a way that wasn't totally unpleasant.

Mom peered at me. "You're blushing."

I just stopped myself from covering my cheeks with my hands. "What? No, I'm not. I'm just . . . it's kind of hot in here."

But Mom was not so easily fooled. "Iz, I know we haven't talked much about boys."

"And we don't need to," I hurried on. "Dex is just a friend."

I didn't realize my mistake until Mom frowned at me. "I thought you said his name was Adam."

"It is," I said, turning away and heading for the door. "Dex is just this other boy. He's in that ghost hunter thing, and you had mentioned that, so it was on my mind. We should go if—"

Mom stood up. "Two boys?" she asked, and I wasn't sure if she was horrified or impressed.

"Friends," I said again. "Nothing else. And didn't you say it was important to blend in? Going on a . . . er, going to a basketball game is totally blending in."

I could tell Mom was struggling between the Brannick part of her that wanted to believe I was doing all of this for the mission—which I *so was*—and the Mom part that suddenly realized she had a teenage daughter. A teenage daughter who was hanging around teenage boys.

She reached out, and I think she was going to lay a hand on my shoulder or something, but in the end, she just let her arm drop to her side. "Izzy, I'm glad you're so dedicated to this, but . . . you have to remember that these kids you're spending time with are just part of a job. You can enjoy spending time with them, but in the end, there isn't any room for them in your life permanently."

I should have just nodded, but instead I said, "But you have friends. Or connections, or whatever. People like Maya. Like whoever found you this house."

Mom frowned slightly. "Those aren't my friends, Izzy, and they're not . . . civilians. They're people who are already wrapped up in this life. People who know about Prodigium and what we do. It's different."

"I understand that," I replied, but Mom just ducked her head to look into my eyes. "Do you? Do you *really*?"

I thought of Dex again, and the way it had been kind of . . . nice sitting with Romy in English class.

But I looked at Mom and said, "Absolutely. A job. Means to an end, all of that. On it."

Mom held my gaze for another beat before sighing. "Okay," she said at last. "Then let me grab my car keys and we'll get you to this game."

CHAPTER 14

The gym was brightly lit, and as I made my way down the hill from the parking lot, I could hear the banging of drums, the squeak of sneakers, and the occasional shout. Inside, it was even louder, and way more packed than I would have expected. Apparently sports are a really big thing around here.

Adam was waiting just inside the door, and I was relieved to see he was wearing more or less the same thing he'd had on at school today. That was one thing I'd gotten right at least. And from the look he gave my hair, I guess that had been right, too. "You look nice," he told me, waving his hand in my general direction.

"Thanks," I said, forcing myself not to shove my hair behind my ears again. "You, um, too."

On Everton and Leslie's first date, he'd taken her to

this fancy restaurant that had ended up burning down by the end of the episode. But before that, the date had looked like fun. I didn't remember them standing around awkwardly, struggling for things to say.

Because that's a TV show, dummy, and this is real life, I reminded myself.

Finally, Adam nodded toward the inside of the gym. "I, uh, usually play in the pep band, but I took the night off. Drums."

"Oh," I said, unsure what else to say. "Drums are . . . loud."

Adam tilted his head to one side, like he couldn't decide if I was being funny or not. Then he just shrugged and said, "Yeah, they are. So do you like basketball?"

I peeked around him, watching as boys in satiny-looking outfits raced up and down the court. "I don't know. I've actually never seen a basketball game before."

Adam's eyes widened. "Whoa, seriously?" From the tone of his voice, you'd think I'd said I'd never, I don't know, been outside before. Breathed air. "Like, you've never been to one, or you've never even seen one on TV?"

"Both," I told him. "We never had a TV before, so . . ."

Now Adam didn't just look surprised, he looked kind of horrified. Maybe that's what made me sound so defensive when I jerked my head toward the court and said, "I've seen stuff *like* this."

Then I remembered that that had been a "party" this coven of dark witches had been throwing, and it hadn't been a ball they'd tossed between them, but a human head.

That little story didn't seem like one I should share with Adam.

He shook his head. "Okay. Well, then I'm glad I could introduce you to your first real basketball game. I mean, our team sucks, but still, right?" He smiled at me, but it didn't reach his eyes, and I knew I wasn't the only one disappointed by the way this "date" was going.

"We should go in," he said, turning toward the gym. I did the same, and promptly collided with a boy.

"Sorry!" I said, reaching up to steady him without thinking.

But since it was Ben McCrary, and I'd just put my hand directly on the shoulder I'd dislocated, he gave a hiss of pain.

"Sorry, sorry, sorry!" I said again, holding my hands up. Ben just stared at me, pale and wide-eyed, and attempted to put as much space as possible between me and him.

"Just-just stay away from me," he sputtered before darting off.

Adam and I watched him go.

"I . . . um, I kind of dislocated his shoulder in P.E.," I said.

Adam was still staring after Ben. "Okay," he said slowly. "I heard that, but I thought it was just a rumor. I mean, no offense, but you're kind of tiny, and Ben McCrary is . . . not."

"I throw a mean dodgeball," was all I could think to say.

Turning back to me, Adam blinked a few times. "So you've never seen a basketball game, you didn't own a TV, and you can dislocate shoulders with dodgeballs?"

I didn't think any of that was meant to be a compliment, but I smiled anyway. "Yup."

Adam took that in. "I'm gonna grab us some Cokes," he finally said, nodding toward the concession booth. "If you want to go on in and grab a seat, I'll find you when I'm done."

"Great," I said, relieved for any suggestion that would put an end to us just standing there.

The game seemed to have just started, but the bleachers were already pretty full. I spotted a few empty spaces in the middle, and was just preparing to wade through the crowd when I glanced up and saw Romy, Anderson, and Dex sitting in the very top row.

They spotted me around the same time, and Romy

waved, gesturing for me to come join them. I picked my way up to the very top of the bleachers, trying not to step on anyone's hand.

Once I was there, Anderson scooted closer to Romy, leaving a space between him and Dex. I squeezed into it, and if my hip bumped Dex's, so what? Everybody was practically sitting in each other's laps as it was.

"Look at you," Dex enthused, leaning forward with his elbows on his knees. "Embracing school spirit, supporting school athletics."

"Yeah," I said, "I'm here—"

But before I could say anything about Adam, Romy leaned across Anderson and said, "It's actually awesome that you showed up. This is kind of an impromptu PMS meeting."

Dex rolled his eyes. "By which Romy means she tricked me and Anderson with the promise of manly things like sports only to foist her ghost-hunting agenda on us once we got here."

"I knew it was a PMS meeting," Anderson offered in his deep voice. "I hate sports."

Dex flung his hand out toward the court. "Well, I don't. I have a very vested interest in watching those dudes in blue beat the ever-loving crap out of the Mary Evans High Hedgehogs."

"Wait, our mascot is the hedgehog?" I asked.

"Up until a few years ago it was a Confederate soldier," Anderson told me. "But then everyone decided that was offensive, so they'd let the student body vote on a new one. That's how we'd ended up with the Mary Evans High Hedgehogs."

He nodded, and for the first time, I saw the mascot. He was standing near the cheerleaders. There'd been some attempt to make him look tough. The hedgehog's quills had been tipped with silver paint to make them look sharp, and his face was twisted into a snarl.

But all the quills and fierce expressions couldn't disguise the fact that, at the end of the day, the mascot was just a six-foot-tall hedgehog.

It was hard to tear my eyes away from that spectacle, but I finally turned to Romy and asked, "So what ghost business are you working on tonight?"

Romy huffed out a breath, ruffling her bangs. "Well, it was supposed to be the séance. My mom got off early tonight, so it was the perfect chance, but when we got here, the stupid trailer was locked."

Looking at me, she added, "I tried texting you like a billion times."

I'd left my phone at home. I still wasn't used to carrying it around, which I obviously needed to get better about. I really didn't want these three doing a séance.

"Romy asked us to break a window," Dex said, "but

I told her I was not prepared to commit a crime, even in the name of science."

"Any chance you'll have another free night soon?" Anderson asked.

Before Romy could answer, Dex said, "Why is Adam Lipinski coming toward us?"

"Oh!" I had kind of forgotten about Adam. But there he was, making his way up the bleachers with two cups in his hands. "He's, um . . . we're here together," I said, and almost as one, Romy, Dex, and Anderson turned to look at me.

"Like, you're on a date?" Romy asked, both eyebrows raised. "And you came to sit with us?"

"He said to find seats," I told her, lifting one shoulder in a shrug.

"He probably meant for the two of you," Dex said, pulling his leg as far away from mine as he could. "And preferably seats that didn't have you wedged between two other guys."

Romy was already at the very end of the row, and Anderson was as close to her as he could get. Dex had a little space on his side, and he scooted away from me, giving Adam just enough room to squeeze in between us.

He handed me my Coke, the cup icy and slick in my hand. "Thanks," I murmured, suddenly unsure and embarrassed again. Was I not supposed to sit with my friends? Was that why Adam's shoulders were all . . . weird?

Taking a sip of my drink, I wondered why it was there were a million books on ghosts and legends and monsters, and nothing useful like, *How to Go On a Normal Date Without Looking Like a Total Spaz.*

"You guys talking ghost stuff?" Adam asked, and next to me, I felt Anderson tense a little.

But Romy leaned over, pleasantly surprised. "We were, actually. Okay, so everyone knows that this place has a ghost, and—"

"And you guys are going to slap on your tinfoil hats and get rid of it?"

Adam said it with a little smile, but it still sounded . . . snide. Mean, even.

Romy's expression hardened and she turned her attention back to the court. "No, we only use our tinfoil hats when there are aliens involved."

On Adam's other side, Dex sighed dramatically and leaned back against the wall, pulling his sunglasses out and slapping them on his face. He then stretched out his long legs, crossing them at the ankle, and folded his hands over his stomach.

Frowning, I leaned forward a little, trying to see past Anderson. "So, since the séance didn't work out, what

PMS business are you dealing with tonight?" I asked Romy.

Her eyes flicked back to Adam for a second before she said, "I just thought with the mutilated doll and everything, we might need to keep an eye on Beth."

"She's cheering tonight," Anderson offered, nodding down at the gym floor. Sure enough, there was Beth standing in a line with a bunch of other girls in green and white, silver pom-poms in her hand. I remembered the doll wearing a rough copy of that same outfit, all mangled and covered in fake blood.

Then next to me, Adam snorted and said, "Oh, that psycho Barbie she found in her locker? Please, that was totally just Ben being a jerk."

"It's more than just that," Romy said, but Adam rattled the ice in his drink and rolled his eyes. "Of course it is. You know, Romy, this ghost hunter thing was cute when we were all in elementary school, but now it just makes you a weirdo. You get that, right?"

"Better a weirdo than a jackass," Dex muttered.

"You're one to talk, dude," Adam fired back, but Dex gave no indication he'd heard him.

"Whatever." Adam stood up and looked down at me. "I'm out of here. Izzy, you coming?"

As I stared up at him, I realized something. I wasn't irritated that Adam had interrupted Romy and screwed up my chances at getting more info. I was irritated because Dex was right. He *was* a jackass.

"No," I told him, curling my hands around the bleacher. "I think I'll stay here."

Adam hadn't been expecting that, I could tell. For a second he looked confused and then, I thought, hurt. But just as quickly, he gave me the same look he'd given Romy. "Okay, fine," he said, walking down a row. "The girl who's never seen TV before probably belongs with these freaks anyway."

With that, he turned and left. The four of us watched him go. Only when he was at the very bottom did Dex say, "Izzy, I don't think your new boyfriend is very nice."

I didn't bother to correct him about Adam being my "boyfriend." So my first date was a total bust, then. But why, watching him walk away, did I feel so . . . I don't know, relieved?

And then something else occurred to me. "Oh, crap. He was supposed to drive me home."

Dex slid his sunglasses down his nose, but before he could say anything, Romy leaned over. "My mom is coming to get me in like an hour. We can drive you home."

"Great," I told her, ignoring the tiny flicker of disappointment. I needed more of a chance to talk to Romy anyway.

There was a sudden shout from the crowd as—I guess—our team scored points. Everyone around us shot to their feet, clapping, but the four of us stayed in our seats.

"Well, Isolde," Dex said over the noise, "how does it feel to have declared for Team Outcast?"

I couldn't help but laugh. "Good," I told him, and I was surprised to discover I meant it.

CHAPTER 15

By the time the game was nearly over, I still didn't really understand basketball, but I did learn that Dex's Nana texted him about every ten minutes any time he was away from the house, that Romy twisted one strand of hair around her finger every time Anderson said something to her, and that Anderson had, up until junior high, actually been a pretty decent basketball player himself.

"Busted my knee waterskiing," he told me, tapping the kneecap in question. "But it was all good. Led to me looking for other ways to spend my time, and then I found Ro—uh, found the club. Ghost hunting seemed like a lot more fun than throwing a stupid ball into a basket, anyway."

"Anderson here is a reformed jock," Dex said. "Which he didn't bother to tell me until we'd already been friends for a month. By then it was too late to shun him, as I should have."

Grinning, Anderson reached over me and thwacked Dex's head, sending his sunglasses tumbling.

Dex gave an outraged cry. "I am affronted! That's it, friendship rescinded."

Anderson just leaned back against the wall and laughed. "Like you said, bro, too late." He turned his gaze down to me. "Of course, if you want to escape this madness while you still can, I wouldn't blame you."

"Hey!" Romy leaned over, laying a proprietary hand on my arm. "We finally have another girl in the group. Please don't run her off just yet."

It was weird watching their easiness with each other, and then seeing them treat *me* like that, too. I'd never really missed having friends—you can't miss something you've never had—but I hadn't realized how, well, awesome they could be, either.

I stood up. "I'm gonna run to the bathroom. Be right back."

Romy looked like she was about to get up, too. "Do you want me to come with you?"

I hesitated, one foot awkwardly lifted over the bleacher below me. "I know where it is," I told her, remembering that I'd seen a girls' room in the gym lobby.

But that must've been the wrong answer, because Romy seemed puzzled. "Oh, okay."

I made my way back down the bleachers, and when I got to the front of the gym, I suddenly saw why Romy had offered to come with me. There were . . . groups of girls huddled outside the bathroom, talking, laughing, some sharing lip gloss. Crap, was that a thing girls who were friends were supposed to do with one another?

Sighing, I turned to the gym doors, noticing that just up the hill there were lights on in the school. There were bathrooms up there, and maybe they wouldn't be so crowded.

It had gotten colder, and I shivered a little as I jogged up toward the school. Luckily, the main breezeway door was unlocked, and I knew the bathroom was just inside, past the lockers.

Flyers pinned to a bulletin board ruffled in the breeze as I yanked open the door. The hall was dark, although there were two rectangles of light from the bathroom doors. I was headed for them when a glow suddenly filled the hall.

For one second I thought someone had just flipped on another light, but no. This wasn't the harsh fluorescent of the hallway lighting, or the dull amber of the bathroom. This was slightly bluish and very, very familiar.

Taking a deep breath, I steeled my nerves and turned around.

Mary Evans floated in the hall just behind me, her long white dress barely brushing the ground. In the picture Romy had shown me, her hair had been styled into some sort of fancy updo, but now it straggled down her back. She didn't speak, but her eyes roamed over me, confusion on her translucent face.

"Hi, Mary," I said, my voice loud in the quiet hall. Okay. This was good. This was confirmation that the ghost stalking Mary Evans High was in fact Mary Evans. But it was hard to feel glad about that when I remembered that the same ghost had nearly killed a guy.

"You need to leave this place."

Her head jerked up, lips curling back in a snarl, and I stepped back. The cold metal of the lockers pressed against my shoulders, and I swallowed hard. "You can't stay—" I started, and then there was a rush of wind as she suddenly surged forward.

It was like I'd been dunked into a tub of ice water. I couldn't see anything but that blue light, and all around me there was this horrible sense of pressure, like hands were pushing on me as hard as they could. But that wasn't the worst part. The worst part was her voice in my mind, shrieking so loudly I could barely make it out. *Pay they have to pay have to pay,* over and over again. Images played behind my eyelids. I saw blood on a microscope, saw Mary's ghostly hand clutched around the base. Then there was a cave, and fire? Something bright, something that *burned*.

And then suddenly the cold and the pressure were gone, the shrieking was silent, and Mary was no longer up against me, all around me.

She hovered there in front of me, chest heaving in and out as though she were still breathing, and she had a frantic look in her eyes. Her mouth opened in a silent scream, head tilting back to cry at the ceiling.

And then she rose up, hovering high over my head before vanishing.

I stood there against the lockers, nearly panting. My knees felt watery, but I made myself stay on my feet. Brannicks don't slump to the floor just because a ghost gets up in their face.

Still, as I pushed myself off the lockers and scrubbed a shaking hand over my mouth, I had to admit that that had not been your run-of-the-mill ghost. I'd seen ghosts before. I'd seen them sad and confused, maybe a little irate. But I'd never seen one as furious as Mary Evans, and I'd certainly never had one try to . . . God, what *had* she been trying to do? It had almost felt like she was trying to climb inside my skin.

Shuddering at that thought, I pushed open the

bathroom door. Inside, I splashed cold water on my face and tried to get my heart rate back to something resembling normal. Reminding myself that coming face to face with Mary Evans was a good thing—hey, now I knew what I was up against—I stepped back into the hallway.

A shadowy figure suddenly appeared in front of me, and with a choked shriek, I reached out and grabbed the front of a shirt, slamming the person against the lockers.

Anderson blinked back at me.

"Oh!" Loosening my fingers, I let him go, smoothing his shirt out with the flat of my hand. "Sorry, you scared me. I startle kind of easily."

Tucking his hair behind his ears, he nodded. "I noticed that." I waited for him to give me the "You Violent Freak" Look Ben McCrary had given me, but to my surprise, Anderson just smiled and said, "I knew you dressed like a ninja, but I didn't think you actually were one."

I laughed. "I didn't hurt you, right?" I asked, but Anderson waved me off.

"No harm, no foul. Romy was looking for you. She took the gym while I headed up here."

"Where's Dex?" I asked before I could stop myself.

Anderson shrugged. "His Nana needed him, so he went home." He frowned, looking more closely at me. "Are you sure you're okay? You're kind of pale."

We opened the breezeway doors, stepping back outside. "Yeah, just . . ." I trailed off, and Anderson nodded.

"Overcome with the majesty of team sports. I understand."

Chuckling, I shrugged. "Something like that." The air didn't feel so cold now that I'd had a ghost trying to snuggle me, and I took a deep breath as we walked down the hill. We had just gotten to the gym when Anderson said, "Hey, Izzy."

I turned and he stood there, hands in his pockets, shoulders hunched. "Uh . . . thanks for being so cool with Romy. I know she likes hanging out with me and Dex, but with you . . . with you being, like, you know, a *girl* and stuff—"

I stopped Anderson before he could actually choke on his tongue. "It's easy to be cool with Romy. She's a cool girl."

Anderson wasn't as good-looking as Dex, but the goofy grin that spread across his face was seriously beautiful. "She's the *coolest* girl," he enthused, and even though I'd just been scared half to death not ten minutes before, I discovered I was grinning, too.

"Who is?" Romy asked, coming up behind him.

Anderson's ears reddened and he kicked at a nonexistent rock. "This girl," he babbled. "This girl who's cool."

Romy raised her eyebrows. "Huh. Informative, Anderson." Tugging at my hand, she started pulling me toward the parking lot. "Come on, Iz, my mom's here."

"Bye, Anderson," I called, waving to him with my free hand.

He gave a sheepish wave back and then turned away.

"So," Romy asked as we stepped into the parking lot, "other than getting ditched by Jerk-Face Adam, how was your first Official Mary Evans High Event?"

I looked back at the school, and even though I couldn't be certain, I thought I saw a flash of blue light.

"Eventful."

CHAPTER 16

Romy's mom drove a minivan, one of those fancy ones with the doors that open on their own and TV screens in the back of every seat. As we clambered into the back, I stepped on one doll, a handful of crackers, and a pile of Legos.

"My siblings are beasts, sorry," Romy said, flopping into her seat.

"They're also four," her mom informed me, catching my eyes in the rearview mirror. Her hair was a few shades darker than mine and pulled up in a haphazard ponytail. A large spot that looked like it might have been grape juice stained her T-shirt from the collar to the middle of her chest.

I noticed the booster seats and looked over at Romy. "You have three siblings?"

"Triplets," she said with a nod. "Three boys. Adorable and evil in equal measure."

"Romy," her mom admonished, and Romy leaned forward, holding on to the back of the seat in front of her. "Mom, I love them, you know I do. But even you have to admit they are five parts cute to five parts holy terror."

I could hear her mom sigh as she glanced down at the dark purple blob on her shirt. "All right, you may not be entirely wrong."

Settling back in her seat, Romy fished a sippy cup lid out from behind her back and tossed it to the floor. "At least I had nine years as an only child. My parents adopted me when I was two," she told me. "I was eleven when the triplets were born, and nothing in my life has ever been quiet again." But even as she said it, there was a kind of softness in her smile, and it twisted something in my chest.

A sensation that only got worse when Romy's mom asked, "What about you, Izzy? Do you have any brothers or sisters?"

"No," I told her around the sudden lump in my throat. "Just me and my mom." What else could I say? "My sister disappeared" was too bizarre and opened the door to too many questions. "My sister died" wasn't true. Or at least I hoped it wasn't. So this was the easiest answer I could give, no matter how much it sucked to say it.

"Your house must be super quiet, then," Romy said. "Now I know where I'm going the next time I need to escape." Her grin was bright.

"Sure," I said, even as I tried to imagine Romy in my house. I'd never had company before. Would Torin behave? Maybe if I talked to him beforehand . . .

"We may need to grab ice cream before taking Izzy home," Romy informed her mom. "She had a rough night."

I jerked my head in Romy's direction. I hadn't told her about seeing Mary's ghost, so what did she—

"Some jerk boy stood her up."

"I didn't get stood up," I said quickly, but Romy waved her hand.

"Okay, so technically you told him to get bent, but that in no way negates the need for ice cream."

"I think I'm good," I told her, but I was smiling.

"Are you sure?" Romy's mom asked. "Because I've taught my daughter well. When boys are jerks, only ice cream will suffice. Or shopping, maybe."

"Ooh!" Romy sat up in her seat. "Yes, shopping. That's what Izzy needs. I mean, not right now, obviously, but sometime in the very near future. No offense," she added, "but while I appreciate this whole goth thing you have going, you could seriously use some color."

Seeing as how tonight Romy was wearing a sweater

such a bright shade of yellow that it practically glowed in the dark, I was a little nervous about what her idea of "color" might mean. But hadn't I just been worrying that my normal Brannick wardrobe wasn't going to hack it at Mary Evans High?

"Okay," I said slowly. "I could . . . maybe get behind a shopping trip."

"Excellent!" Romy said. "Next week. Mom, can you take us? On Thursday?"

"I can," her mom agreed before catching my gaze in the rearview mirror. "Romy tells me you've joined her club. Are you into all things supernatural, too, Izzy?"

"You could say that," I told her. "Mostly I was just excited the school had something as cool as a Paranormal Management Society."

"Well, I'm glad you joined. Romy could use some girlfriends. Not that Anderson and Dex aren't nice boys; it's just that it's so hard for Romy to find girls who share her interests."

"Mom," Romy said, embarrassed.

I looked over at Romy, and felt guilt wash over me. I liked her, I did. But it wasn't like I was being her friend just because she was a cool person. I was . . . using her.

What was it Mom has said? *Remember, don't get too close. These people are a means to an end.*

That thought was still bothering me when Romy's

mom pulled up in our driveway, but I tried not to let it show. Instead, I put on my brightest voice, told Romy I'd see her tomorrow, thanked her mom for the ride, and went inside.

Mom was sitting at the kitchen table when I came in, one of those ancient books in front of her. She barely glanced up as I took the seat across from her. "How did it go?"

I shrugged. "Okay. I saw the ghost we're dealing with, and let me tell you, she is one seriously unhappy chick."

"Dangerous?" Mom asked, linking her fingers on top of her book.

"I can handle it," I said automatically, even as I remembered just how full of rage Mary had been. I thought about asking Mom if she knew much about ghosts possessing people—if that had been what the whole pushing thing had been about—but decided against it. Mom needed to think I could do this on my own.

Because I could.

So before she could ask me anything else, I said, "I think I cemented my friendship with the ghost hunter kids, but . . ."

"But?" Mom prompted.

Sighing, I propped my chin in my hand. "I think I'm really bad at dating."

Mom huffed out a laugh and turned her attention back to her book. "Is it awful that I'm kind of thrilled about that?"

I wanted to ask her more about it. Like, had it been wrong to sit with PMS? Was Adam being a jerk, or was that just teenage boys? I mean, sure, Dex didn't seem like that, but he *wasn't* a regular teenage boy, and . . .

"Did Finn ever date? When you guys had those longer jobs that took a few weeks. Was there ever, like, a guy or anything?"

Surprised, Mom looked up. "I . . . I honestly don't know. She never mentioned anyone."

If we found Finley—*when* we found her—I would ask her.

There were a couple of pens on the table, and I picked one up, poking at Mom's book. "So this research. What is it about?"

Curling her fingers around the edges of the volume, Mom scooted it away, just the tiniest bit. "Nothing you need to worry about. Just something I'm looking into for Maya."

She inhaled sharply through her nose, the same way Finn always did right after she told a lie. My chest tightened, and I fought the urge to yank the book back, to see for myself what Mom was so interested in. It had to be about Finley. But if it was, why wouldn't she tell me, let me help her?

Because she's afraid you're going to screw it up, a voice hissed in my head. *Because if you had just gone into the house with Finley that night, she might still be here.*

Blinking against a sudden stinging in my eyes, I just nodded. "Okay."

The silence that hung over the table was threatening to turn awkward, so I cleared my throat and said, "You know, the only part of the Mary Evans things that doesn't make sense to me is the frog and the Barbie."

Mom rested her elbows on the book in front of her. "You're right. There are plenty of stories about ghosts attacking people, but that level of physical manipulation . . . it would take a lot of energy. That's not just wielding a weapon; that's planning."

I nodded, drumming my fingers on the table. "It seems kind of advanced for a ghost."

"Advanced, yes, but not unheard of."

Mom and I both jumped as Torin's voice floated through the kitchen. I glanced around, wondering where he could be, and my eyes landed on the clock above the stove. It was framed in a beveled mirror, and even though all the little pieces of Torin were hard to make out, I could still see him in there.

"Torin, you know you're supposed to keep to your

mirror," Mom said, getting up and heading for the clock. She lifted it off the wall, and Torin made an aggrieved sound.

I stood up from the table, leaning one hand against it. "Have you seen something like this before?"

Mom stopped, the mirrored clock held out from her body. I couldn't see Torin's face, but I heard him clearly when he answered, "Only once. My coven raised a particularly nasty ghost. On their own, spirits are usually harmless, but if they've been summoned forth by any type of magic, well. Completely different kettle of fish."

Lowering the clock to the table, Mom considered that. "So you think a witch or a warlock could have somehow raised this spirit?"

"Possibly." Mom had put the clock facedown, so Torin's voice came out muffled. "Or, at the very least, powered it up. Isolde mentioned that there had been very basic haunting activity at this school for quite some time. So why now? What changed in the past few months to turn an ordinary specter into something that can perform such feats as securing a dead frog to a door, or mutilating a toy?"

I chewed my lip. How long had Dex been in Ideal? It couldn't be a coincidence that just when this guy, who was clearly *something*, showed up, Mary Evans had become Uber-Ghost.

But Mom just shrugged. "Well, it's not like it matters. Powerful or not, ghosts are easy to dispose of. And we just have a few more days until the full moon. Izzy will get rid of it, and that will be that."

Except that I wasn't sure that *would* be that. If someone was raising ghosts, what was to stop them from raising another one once Mary Evans was gone? For just a second, it was on the tip of my tongue to tell Mom about Dex. But what if I did, and she decided this case was too big for me after all, and just decided to take it over herself?

I glanced at the pile of books on the table—Mom's super-secret "research" that she still wouldn't tell me about.

If she was going to keep her secrets, I would keep mine.

CHAPTER 17

"Here." Romy added a sweater to the pile in my arms. "Redheads look good in green."

I cast a doubtful look at the sweater. "This . . . doesn't look like green."

The shade should've been called "Radioactive" or maybe "Noxious." That had been one of our vocabulary words this morning.

Frowning, Romy reached into the rack and pulled out a black skirt. "Here, Ninja Lady," she said, tossing it to the top of my stack. "You can wear it with black."

We'd been shopping for over an hour, and Romy had already talked me into a pink blouse, two pairs of jeans that were *not* black, three T-shirts in various shades of purple, and even a yellow sundress. "First day of spring, if I don't see you rocking this, I'm going to be very disappointed," Romy had said when she'd shoved it into my arms.

"Deal," I'd replied, even as a little voice inside my head reminded me that I wouldn't be in Ideal in the spring.

Now I gently put back both the green sweater and the black skirt. "I think we're set, Romy. My mom's credit card can only take so much."

Romy heaved a huge sigh and ran her fingers longingly over the green sweater. "What if I bought it, and then you could borrow it sometimes?"

I laughed. "Clearly, you and that sweater were meant to be."

Once we left the store, we still had nearly half an hour to kill before her mom was due to pick us up. Ideal had one mall, and while it wasn't exactly upscale, there were a few nice stores, and I had to admit, the smells wafting from the food court were pretty tempting. But rather than head that way, Romy steered us toward a particularly sad-looking toy store.

"You know, I'm actually all stocked up on My Little Ponies," I told her as she dragged me through the entrance. Romy rolled her eyes.

"First of all, no girl can ever have enough My Little Ponies. That's just science. But secondly, we're not here for those. I need to get a new Ouija board. The one we have is all scratched up and smells like school."

Oh, right. The séance was coming up. I'd promised Mom I'd stop it, and what had I been doing instead? Going to basketball games. Shopping for clothes.

"Are we really gonna do the séance thing?" I asked as Romy moved toward the board game section.

"Um, yeah. Whenever I get another free night, that is." Walking her fingers down stacks of boxes, she finally found the one she was looking for. "Aha!"

As she pulled the Ouija board from the shelf, I shifted my bags to my other arm and put a hand on the box. "Look, I love a good séance, but Ouija boards are so old-fashioned. Isn't there something more . . . technical we could use?"

Romy didn't take her hand away from the box, but she did frown thoughtfully. "Like what?"

"I don't know. Didn't Anderson just get a new EMP reader? Maybe let him use that. And, I mean, honestly, Romy, do you trust Dex with a Ouija board?"

It was the right thing to say. Romy visibly flinched. "Ugh. You're right. He'll just push it around to say inappropriate things and then swear it was Mary Evans, 'that saucy wench' or something."

I couldn't help but laugh. "Yes. Yes, he will do exactly that."

The box slid back onto the shelf. "Anderson *has* been

wanting to try out his EMP recorder. See if we can record any ghostly energy spikes. And even Dex can't screw that up." Then she wrinkled her nose. "Except he probably could."

I tried not to sigh with relief as Romy turned away from the board games. "Awesome," I said. "Besides, I've been wanting to see what kind of gear Anderson has." Mostly to make sure it didn't actually work, but I didn't tell Romy that.

We left the toy store, making our way down the mall toward the entrance. Some '80s soft rock ballad was playing, and a harried-looking mom walked past us, a little kid tugging on her hand. A few feet away, there was a big fountain splashing turquoise-colored water, a couple of girls sitting on the edge, giggling together.

"Are you an alien?"

"What?" I asked, turning to Romy. She was smiling, but there was genuine curiosity in her dark eyes.

"You're looking around the mall like you've never been in one before. And sometimes you look around the school that way, too."

"Oh," I said, heat rising to my face. So much for "blending in."

"Where did you live before this?" Romy asked, maneuvering around a couple of old ladies power walking.

"Tennessee." Immediately, I wondered if I should add more, so I hurried on. "I went to a really small all-girls school, so, yeah, this is all a little new to me."

That apparently satisfied Romy. "Okay. So why did your mom pull you out of that place and move you to freaking Ideal, Mississippi, a.k.a. The Most Boring Town on Earth?"

"Oh, I don't know," I said, swinging my bag. "My last school didn't have *ghosts*. Or ghost hunters for that matter." I thought about *Ivy Springs*, the way Leslie and her identical cousin, Lila, would sometimes laugh together and link arms and bump hips and stuff. I wondered if I should attempt a hip bump now.

But Romy was a lot taller than me, so my hip would just hit her thigh, and . . . yeah, we could skip that bit.

Suddenly her entire face brightened and she grabbed my arm. "Oh! Speaking of ghost hunters . . ."

She reached into her purse, fishing around for something. "Remember when you asked if there was some connection between Beth and Mr. Snyder? You know, something that wasn't gross and illegal?"

"Right," I said as I dodged a couple of kids with balloons tied around their wrists.

"Well, I did a little Internet sleuthing and found this." She pulled a folded-up piece of paper out and handed it to me. It was a mention on the Mary Evans High

Web site. The title read, MEHS CELEBRATES AN 'IDEAL' HISTORY.

"So last year, the school did this big thing about the history of the town and how many students and faculty had had family here when Ideal was founded. And check it." She pointed at the picture. "There's Beth, there's Snyder."

I recognized Beth easily enough, also noting that Adam and Anderson were in the picture. Mr. Snyder, a dark-haired guy who looked to be around thirty, was the only adult.

"I mean, it's not much, but it's something, right?" Romy was watching me with big dark eyes.

"Yeah," I agreed, studying the photo.

They have to pay, Mary had said. Thought. Felt. Whatever all of that shrieking in my head had been. But Mary had frozen to death, according to the legend. A crappy way to go, but not exactly something you could blame other people for. But what if Mary did hold someone responsible and was seeking revenge through that person's descendants? Stranger things had happened.

"I still wonder why now, though. A hundred years she's been dead, and she just now decides to go crazy?" I glanced over at Romy.

She shrugged. "Who knows why ghosts do things?" Then she grinned. "Ooh, or maybe our town is, like, built over the underworld! And psychic evil energy is just now leaking into Ideal." She mulled that over like a little kid making a Christmas list. "Man, think of all the ghosts we'd have then," she said wistfully, and I nearly laughed.

I wasn't sure how anyone could be excited about their town potentially being a portal to Hell, but I clapped a hand on Romy's shoulder and said, "We can only hope."

CHAPTER 18

A few days later, I sat at the dinner table with Mom, twirling spaghetti around my fork. "So Mrs. Steele was telling us that Macbeth was a real person who really killed a king, but that the witches and the ghosts were all made up. Which, I mean, obviously they weren't."

I took a bite of pasta, chewing and swallowing before saying, "It's lame. I think everyone would be a lot more interested in the play if they knew how real it all was. Maybe I'll write something about that in my essay."

Mom gave me a weird look, so I quickly amended. "Not that I'd mentioned the witches and ghosts being real, but something about the way supernatural—"

"It's the last night of the month, Izzy," Mom said,

shaking her head. "You won't need to write that essay."

I lowered my fork. "Right."

Pushing her plate away, Mom rested her elbows on the table. "You hadn't forgotten, had you?"

Of course I hadn't. I just . . . maybe hadn't thought of leaving Ideal so soon after the banishing was done. Which was stupid. If Mary's ghost was put to bed, what reason did we have to stay?

Mom got up from the table, carrying her plate to the sink. "In any case, tonight's the night. I picked up a few canisters of salt at the grocery store. They're in the pantry."

Dishes clattered, and Mom turned on the faucet. "You did a good job," she said, her back to me. "You were able to figure out who the ghost was, and now you'll banish her, and no one's gotten hurt. No one except that boy in your P.E. class, at least. You want me to come with you tonight?"

"I think I can manage pouring some salt onto some dirt," I said, hating how petulant I sounded.

Mom must not have liked it either, because she sighed and turned to face me. "Not every case is glamorous, Isolde. Some of them are just . . . pouring salt. Saying a few words. Moving on."

"I guess," I replied. In the silence that followed, I could hear the steady *plink-plink* of water dripping from the sink.

Mom turned around. "Have you liked school?"

Surprised, I lifted my shoulders in a shrug. "Kind of," I told her. "I mean, I've only been there a month, and it hasn't exactly been a thrill a minute. Are all high schools so . . . dull?"

Mom's mouth quirked in what might have been a smile. "Mine was."

My fork skidded across the spaghetti. "You went to high school? Like, a regular one?" As far as I knew, no Brannick ever spent much time in the human world. We were too busy training and fighting and saving everyone from unholy evil.

"For a little while," Mom said. "Me and my sister. Our mom was working a job in California that ended up taking a lot of time. She thought it would be a good idea for us to at least try school while we were there."

"Did you like it?"

"That's like asking if I liked all my teeth pulled out through my nose," she said, and while I wanted to laugh, that sounded so much like something Finn would've said that my chest felt tight. "So that's a no, then," I finally managed to say, and Mom gave a dry chuckle.

"It wasn't all bad. I liked history, and there was

something . . . I don't know, novel about it, I guess. It wasn't for me, but I was grateful for the experience. Eventually." She hesitated again, like she couldn't decide if she should say anything else. Then she said, "It let me know what I didn't want."

Her eyes met mine across the kitchen. "And I'm sorry, Iz. For you and Finn. I should've let the two of you have a choice, too. Before now."

"You would let us . . . choose not to be Brannicks?" I asked. It seemed like the most impossible thing in the world. This was who we were, what we were born to do. You didn't just get to reject your entire bloodline and sacred calling.

But Mom nodded. "If it's what you wanted."

The words hung between us until finally Mom cleared her throat. "Anyway, yes, school is boring. And soul sucking. But everyone should go through it, even if it's only for a little while."

"So what now?" I asked then, pushing my plate away. "I pour some salt and we pack up and leave?" The idea should've filled me with jubilation. A month of regular high school was more than enough for anyone, and it would be nice to get back to our house. And sure, I'd miss Romy and Anderson. And Dex. But Mom was right: we didn't have room for friends in our lives.

Of course, there was one mystery that still needed

solving. One thing that might keep us in Ideal a little longer. "But if someone is raising ghosts, what's to stop him or her from just raising another one once we salt the grave?"

Mom pinched the bridge of her nose between her thumb and forefinger. "Good point."

I swallowed. Now or never. "Also, um, one of the kids in PMS . . . er, the ghost-hunting thing. He's Prodigium."

When Mom's brows shot up, I faltered a little. "Or at least I think he is."

"Think?" Mom repeated. "Iz, you always know when someone is Prodigium. You even know what type."

"Usually, yeah," I said, tucking my hair behind my ears. "But this guy . . . I can't tell. I didn't even know he was Prodigium until he touched me." Mom's brows went even higher, and I quickly added, "On the hand. In a handshake. No bathing suit areas involved."

She studied me for a long moment before saying, "Are you sure it was magic you felt, and not . . . other things?"

"Yes!" I exclaimed, throwing up my hands. "God, why does everyone keep saying that?"

Hand on one hip, Mom stared me down. "Who is everyone?"

I swallowed. "Just . . . just Torin."

"So you told Torin about this boy being Prodigium, but not me?"

It sounded kind of bad when she put it like that. "I just . . . I wasn't sure it was anything, and I didn't want to bug you while you were working."

"Isolde, I do not know how many times I have to tell you this, but Torin is useless more often than not. If you need advice or help with something, you come to me, and be honest and upfront."

"Like you're being with all your 'research'?" As soon as the words were out of my mouth, I regretted them.

Movements stiff, Mom walked to the pantry and pulled out two canisters of salt. "This should be enough," she said, handing them to me. "Go salt the grave, stop the haunting, and get back here. Then we can talk more about this Prodigium boy."

"Fine," I said, taking the salt more roughly than I'd intended. Mom didn't say anything, though, and I headed upstairs to get my backpack.

Torin was already chilling out in my mirror when I opened the door. He brightened when I came in. "Oh, good, you're here. Is it time to watch a new episode of *Ivy Springs*? If Everton asks Rebecca to the prom instead of Leslie—"

"I don't have time tonight," I told him, shoving the salt into my bag.

If I hadn't known better, I would've sworn that Torin seemed hurt. "You never have time anymore. I've barely seen you in the past few weeks, and what on earth could be more important than *Ivy Springs*?"

"Ghost busting," I answered.

"Ah," he said, nodding toward the backpack. "That explains it. And here I thought you perhaps had a sodium problem."

I picked up one of the ponytail holders by my bed and flicked it at him. It bounced harmlessly off the glass. "After you get back from destroying the ghost, then can we bemoan Everton and Leslie's tragic love?" he asked, picking at the lace on his cuffs.

"Sure," I said, but he frowned.

"Why do you seem so sad, Isolde?"

"I'm not," I answered immediately. "I'm just . . . Mom and I are having a thing right now."

Torin snorted. "You and Aislinn are always having 'a thing.' I think it's more than that." Leaning forward, he squinted at me. "Isolde, are you . . . are you saddened to be leaving this wretched place so soon?"

"No," I replied quickly. Too quickly. Torin settled back against my bed in the mirror, a smug smile on his face.

"You *are*," he said. "You don't want to leave. One mere sample of the cornucopia that is a regular American high school, and you have developed a taste for it."

Rolling my eyes, I shoved my arms through the sleeves of a black jacket. "You've completely cracked."

Scowling, Torin folded his arms over his chest. "You know I don't appreciate mirror jokes."

Doing my best to look contrite, I picked up my backpack. "I'm sorry, Torin. I'll try to *reflect* on my actions."

"All right, now you are just being mean."

He was still grumbling when I left, which should've made me smile. Annoying Torin was one of my favorite pastimes. But it was hard to grin when his words still sat in my stomach like a rock.

One of the great things about the tininess of Ideal was how easy it was to walk to everything. The graveyard where Mary Evans was buried was only a few blocks from my house. So even with all my deep thoughts weighing me down, I was there in no time.

Most people think graveyards are creepy, but I'd been in enough of them over the years that this one just felt kind of . . . homey. I made my way past the newer graves, into the older section of the cemetery. Mary Evans's grave wasn't hard to find. There was a huge marble statue marking her final resting place.

I paused, reading the inscription: MARY ANNE EVANS 1890–1908 FOREVER OUR ANGEL, FOREVER AT REST.

"I really hope so," I murmured as I pulled my

backpack off my shoulders. I grabbed one of the salt canisters and pried open its funnel. The entire grave would have to be covered with salt in order to bring her spirit back and lock her in.

"Sorry to ground you like this, Mary," I whispered. I had just started pouring when a voice said, "Fancy meeting you here."

I whirled around.

Dex.

CHAPTER 19

I froze, but the salt kept pouring out of the nozzle, making a little pyramid on top of the grave. For a long beat, Dex just watched it trickle out.

Once the container was empty, he looked at me. "Soooo . . . whatcha doin'?"

"What are you doing?" I fired back. The same night I go to banish a ghost that may have been raised by magic, Dex, who may be Prodigium, shows up. That was a little too coincidental for me.

"I followed you," he said, like that was every bit as normal as me and my salt. "I was on my way home from the store, and I saw you, so thought I'd see what the Illustrious Isolde Brannick was up to."

With as much dignity as I could muster, I spread the little pile of salt over the dirt with the tip of my shoe.

"You can't just go around following people," I told Dex as I tossed the empty salt carton into my backpack. "It's creepy. And inappropriate."

"Says the girl pouring salt onto graves."

I glared at him. "This is . . . part of my religion."

Smirking, Dex put his hands in his coat pockets. "Oh, so you belong to the Crazy Salt Freak Church?"

"It's an Irish-Celtic thing," I tried, but Dex just shook his head.

"I don't know whether to be more insulted that you're lying to me, or that you apparently think I'm some kind of idiot. Also, it hasn't escaped my knowledge that this"—he nodded at the tombstone—"is the final resting place of one Mary Evans. The very same Mary Evans who Anderson wants to EMP, and Romy wants to Ouija."

My mind raced, trying to come up with some plausible explanation. Unfortunately, all I could think was, *What would Leslie do if Everton caught her pouring salt on graves?* Since I was pretty sure the answer was *cry prettily*, I rejected that idea and decided to go for what Mom always said: *When you're caught in a lie, stick as close to the truth as you can.*

"Ouija boards don't work."

Dex rocked back on his heels, still grinning. "That a fact?"

"I'm just saying, I don't think that anything made by

Milton Bradley is much good for contacting the dark side, that's all."

"Meanwhile, the Morton Salt girl is totally connected to the forces of evil. That would explain her coat."

"Salt destroys evil spirits. I . . . I read it on the Internet this afternoon."

Nudging the salt pile with his foot, Dex shrugged and said, "Okay. I can buy that. But then why come out here by yourself? Why not meet with us and let PMS get their Salt Warrior on?"

Ugh, was he secretly a member of the FBI? I had never met anyone who asked so many questions.

"I thought you guys would think it was dumb."

At that, Dex threw his head back and gave a barking laugh. "For God's sake, Izzy, we call ourselves PMS. And trust me, your salt theory is no dumber than the time Romy investigated a Civil War graveyard with tinfoil on her head."

"That . . . actually happened?" I'd just assumed they were joking.

Dex nodded. "Or when Anderson spent every penny he made mowing lawns for two summers on a special tape recorder that was supposed to capture ghostly voices." His eyes met mine. They were very blue and . . . twinkly. "Besides, your weirdness is why I like you so much."

I didn't know what to say to that, but luckily, he

didn't seem to need a reply. "So. You've made this lovely little salt pile. What can I do?"

"You can go home," I told him, but he was already taking off his jacket—another peacoat, but this one was deep purple in the moonlight—and laying it gently over one of the angels' outspread wings. Then he knelt down and started spreading the salt with his hands. He had pretty hands, I decided. Thin and long-fingered and deli-cate. Like a pianist. I'd never really thought about boys' hands before, but looking at Dex's made me feel warm and shivery all at the same time.

Grudgingly, I knelt down next to him and pulled the other canister of salt out of my backpack. "Just . . . keep doing that. You have to cover the entire grave with salt to confine the spirit." Dex lifted his head, and I added, "I mean, that's what the Internet said."

Satisfied, Dex went back to the salt. After a while, he moved to the foot of the grave, pouring it there.

"This is fun," he said. "Weird and disturbing and possibly illegal, but still fun."

"Is it okay if we don't tell Romy and Anderson about this?"

He grinned at me. "Absolutely. Now we've formed our own splinter cell of PMS."

Leaning forward, he lowered his voice to a conspira-torial whisper. "We've gone rogue."

I made a sound almost like a giggle. Not that I did giggle. Brannicks aren't gigglers. Dex and I spent the next few minutes pressing the salt into the grass. We didn't say anything else, but there was something nice about the silence. It reminded me of when Finn and I used to hang out in the War Room, me reading, her sharpening weapons. Just being with her had been . . . comforting. Nice. That's how it felt now with Dex, even doing something as bizarre as sealing a ghost in its grave.

Then we reached for the same tiny mound of salt and our hands brushed. This time, Dex didn't apologize, but as soon as his skin touched mine, I felt that little hum. That reminder that Dex wasn't a normal boy. That I didn't know what he was. And the more time I spent with him, the less sure I was that even he knew what he was.

Sobered, I stood up, backing away from him a little bit. "Okay," I said, my voice unsteady. "That's . . . that."

"Excellent. So no more ghosts, no more science teachers getting brained, and lockers that open mysssterioooously," Dex said, wiggling his fingers at me. I almost made that giggle sound again, but I stopped myself. Confusion flashed across Dex's face, and he stuffed his hands into his pockets. "Well," he said, but he didn't add anything else.

Suddenly the silence between us wasn't comfortable

so much as awkward. I dusted my hands off on the back of my pants. "I better head home. Mom'll be pissed if I'm out late."

Dex twisted his wrist, glancing at his watch. "It's not even eight. Are your parents Amish?"

"My mom is just . . . strict."

"So is my Nana, but I get to stay out until at least nine. And I don't know about you, but all this salting the earth has me craving fries. You wanna go grab something to eat?"

Eating food together. At night. I didn't even need Everton and Leslie to tell me that was a date. Or had this been a date? We'd laughed and had fun and touched hands. That felt kind of . . . date-y even if it was on top of a grave.

But he was smiling at me again, and now that he mentioned it, I hadn't eaten much dinner. "Can you get me home by nine?"

His grin widened. "Isolde, my friend, I can get you back by quarter 'til." He held out his hand to help me to my feet. "Shall we?"

I only hesitated for a second before taking it, and this time, when a pulse shot through me, I wasn't a hundred percent sure it was only magic I was feeling.

CHAPTER 20

Several minutes later, Dex and I were seated in a bright red vinyl booth at a place that called itself the Dairee Kween.

"What's with the misspelling?" I'd asked when we'd pulled up.

"It used to be an actual Dairy Queen, but the corporate office made them close it down after a major rat outbreak in the kitchen. So the owners just reopened it, but changed the spelling to keep from getting sued."

"That . . . does not make me want to eat here."

Dex laughed. "The rat thing was like thirty years ago, according to my Nana. And it's probably just a rumor anyway."

He might have been right, but I made a note to skip the burgers. Besides, it's not like I was ever going to eat here again. Mary Evans's ghost was put to rest, and Mom and I would be moving on. Which was awesome and great and not at all sad-making.

"This is better than our regular PMS meetings," Dex said once we had our food. "Those are sadly lacking in fries, I've found." He reached past me for the ketchup. "And desecrating graves is a surprisingly fun bonding activity. I only defile the dead with my closest friends."

"So we're friends," I said hesitantly, swirling a french fry in ketchup. Dex snagged a fry from my plate and popped it into his mouth.

"Yes," he said, chewing. "And now that I've stolen food from you, it's official. You and me, friends for life."

"Good," I said. "I . . . I like being friends with you."

"Same." He made my favorite grin, the one that was surprisingly goofy for such a handsome guy.

Wait a second. I'd known him for a few weeks. How did I have a *favorite grin* of his?

Our eyes met and held, and it was like there was this . . . pulse between us. For a second I thought it was just Dex's magic or power or whatever it was that I was picking up on. But it didn't feel like that. It felt—

Dex's phone beeped, and as he looked down at it, the moment was lost. Which, to be honest, was kind of a relief. "My Nana," he sighed. "Why oh why did I ever teach that woman to text?" As his thumbs moved over the keypad, I pretended to be super-interested in my fries. Really, I was studying him.

He certainly didn't seem like a guy with anything to hide, but why had he been at Mary's grave? It couldn't just be a coincidence that he'd shown up when he did. Had he really followed me, or was there more to it than that? I needed to get closer to Dex.

The thought immediately sent a flutter through me, and I dropped my eyes back to my plate. Not close to him like *that*. Close in the general Finding Out Information way. "There," he said, sliding his phone into his bag. "Apparently my curfew has been lengthened by an hour since I'm with you." He waggled his eyebrows. "I told her I was with a lady who is quite the good influence on me."

"You *need* a good influence," I told him, smiling a little.

Dex sat back in his chair, impressed. "Isolde Brannick. Are you flirting with me?"

I tossed a fry at his head. It bounced off his shoulder, and he winced theatrically, pressing his hand to his clavicle. "Easy, slugger! In your hands, a french fry is a deadly weapon."

"No, I'm only deadly with dodgeballs," I said, and he laughed.

"Flirting and joking! Within a few minutes of each other! Is this the side of Isolde that only her friends get to see?"

He was teasing, but it gave me the opening I'd been hoping for. "Yup. And speaking of . . ." I ventured. "Friends . . . they can . . . they can tell each other stuff, right? I just mean . . . if you had some kind of secret, or something you hadn't ever told anyone, you could tell me. No matter . . . no matter what it was."

Oh, smooth, Izzy. Seriously. Why didn't I just grab him and yell, "TELL ME WHAT KIND OF MAGICAL POWERS YOU HAVE!" By the end of my little stuttering speech, I was blushing and Dex was frowning.

"A secret?" he asked, puzzled. Then his face suddenly cleared, and he shook his head. "Oh, right. Because of all the purple."

"Purple?"

"The clothes, I mean," he said, gesturing to his coat. "I know that I'm fashionable and well-groomed, and yes, I have been known to rock the occasional man-bracelet."

He lifted his wrist, jangling the bracelet I'd noticed earlier. I could see now that it was plain silver, just a series of links.

"But," Dex continued, dragging another one of my fries through ketchup, "I also like ladies. And not as shopping buddies, but in the carnal sense." His tone was light as always, but he wouldn't meet my eyes. Not to mention, that spiel was so smooth, he had to have done it before.

I'd only thought I was blushing before. Now my face was probably the same color as the tabletop. "Dex, I wasn't asking if you were . . . I didn't think you . . ."

"Oh." He took a drink of his soda. "Then you were just asking me to spill some . . . nonspecific secret?"

I shook my head. "Forget it." This was obviously getting us nowhere, so I decided to try a new subject. "Tell me more about your Nana."

Dex's face immediately brightened. "Basically, she is the bestest Nana in all the land. Bakes cookies, knits afghans, and lets me hang out past curfew with lovely ladies such as yourself. You should meet her someday. She'd love you."

Was meeting Nana a serious thing? It kind of felt like it. I *really* needed to get those magazines. Making a mental note to stop by the drugstore I'd noticed on my way to the graveyard, I nodded. "I'd like that. And your parents, are they also the bestest?"

If Dex's face had gone all shiny at the mention of his Nana, bringing up his parents had the opposite effect. His shoulders slumped a little, and something flickered in his eyes. "They died when I was little. Just me and my Nana for a while now." He took a long sip of his Coke, rattling ice in the cup. I had the sense that it was less about being thirsty and more about dropping the subject.

"My dad died when I was little, too," I heard myself say, and Dex lowered his cup.

This wasn't part of my cover; this was the real deal, but he had shared something with me, so it felt right to return the favor. "He, uh, was a soldier." That was literally all I knew about my dad. Men don't tend to stick around in the Brannick family.

Dex nodded slowly. "Sucks, doesn't it?"

I hadn't known my dad, so I didn't miss him the way I missed Finn, but still I replied, "It does."

A silence fell over the table, and I mentally kicked myself. I was supposed to be getting information out of him, not sharing personal feelings.

Ignoring the tiny voice that said maybe my interest in Dex was less than Brannick-y, I reached out and took his wrist. This time I was prepared for the little buzz that went through me. "You know, I actually like this man-bracelet," I said, turning his wrist for a better look. I hoped it came off as jokey and kind of flirty, but really I was inspecting it for . . . well, anything. Maybe there were runes or something carved into the links.

Preening a little, Dexter leaned closer to me. "That's because you're a woman of taste. My Nana gave this to me. I have very strict instructions never to take it off."

I looked up sharply at that. "Seriously? Never? Why?" For the first time since I'd met him, Dex seemed a little uncomfortable. Taking his hand back, he shrugged. "Superstitious thing, I think. Nana, like you, has a touch of the Irish in her." He turned his wrist, the silver gleaming in the fluorescent lights. "Supposed to be lucky, I guess." And then he flashed that grin again. "And clearly it has been lucky, because I was wearing it when I met you." He grabbed another fry from my plate. "My new best friend."

In spite of myself, I laughed. "Oh, so now we're best friends?"

He nodded very seriously. "Three fries I've stolen from you. That cements it."

By the time Dex drove me home, I was thinking less about his bracelet and his Nana and whatever it was I felt when I touched him and more about how nice it was talking and laughing with a boy. Leslie and Everton didn't seem to do much laughing. Mostly they were either crying or angsting or making overly dramatic declarations of love to one another. That had seemed kind of fun on the show, but I thought maybe this was better.

But those kinds of thoughts were pointless and stupid (and I clearly needed to stop watching *Ivy Springs*). *It's a job*, I reminded myself as Dex opened the passenger door for me. *He is a job. You don't get to think things like how soft his hair looks. Or how nice his eyes are.*

Dex walked me as far as the front door, and when he stopped there, my heart pounded in my throat. Oh, God, this was the part where kissing happened. I may never have been on a date, but I'd watched enough TV and read enough books to know that when you eat food with a boy and then he takes you to your door, kissing will occur.

And I was in no way ready for that. Kissing was another one of those things I'd meant to do more research on, just in case. Like, how did you know which way to turn your head? And what about teeth placement? What if there was a spit issue? Should I have taken Torin up on his offer to help me practice? Trying to keep the panic off my face, I turned toward Dex. "Right. So. Good night, then."

He gave a little bow. "Until tomorrow, Fair Isolde."

And then he leaned forward.

My heart was in my ears, and my hands were shaking. Okay, I could do this. It was just lips. Just lips pressing together, hopefully without spit. And tongues . . . tongues . . . Okay, actually, no. I could *not* do this.

I was just about to pull back when Dex reached out and . . . ruffled my hair. "Sleep tight!" he called cheerfully as he jogged down the front steps.

"Um. You too," I replied, but I was so dazed that I

didn't get that out until he was already in the car, pulling away.

Was he going to ruffle my hair all along? Had I just imagined the way he'd looked at my mouth? Or had he seen the naked panic on my face and changed his mind?

I walked into the house and turned to face the little mirror in the hallway. At least that confirmed that, yup, hair and face, totally the same shade. "Magazines," I whispered firmly at myself. "Tomorrow."

Torin's face suddenly appeared, frowning. "Are you talking to me? And why are you all beet colored?"

Luckily, Mom walked around the corner, and Torin immediately vanished. "That took longer than I'd expected," she said, drying her hands on a dish towel.

"I ran into that kid. The one I think is Prodigium. We, uh, grabbed some food."

"And?" Mom asked expectantly.

"And I still don't know what he is." Taking a deep breath, I pushed my shoulders back. "So I wanna stay. A little longer. Just until I find out." After all, there was a chance this whole thing wasn't really over, no matter all the salt thrown on Mary's grave. If Dex's Possible Prodigium Powers had had anything to do with raising her ghost, I needed to know.

Frowning, Mom tossed the towel into the kitchen. "Do you think he's anything dangerous?"

181

My knees felt watery and my heart was racing. Yeah, Dex was dangerous, all right, but not in the way Mom meant. I gave her my best Tough Chick Grimace. "No. But if he is, I'll take care of it."

She watched me for a long time, so long that I was afraid she was about to say no. Instead, she shrugged. "Okay, then. This one is all yours."

I told myself that the relief flooding through me had everything to do with Mom's trusting me, and nothing at all to do with getting to stay in Ideal.

"But you just get one more month," Mom said. "No more. Anything longer than that can be dangerous for us."

"Right," I said, nodding. Mom never liked to work long jobs. The way she saw it, the longer you were in a place, the more you were expected to make connections, friends even. And Brannicks could never afford that. Too many questions.

"Mom," I said, scuffing my toe against the linoleum. "About earlier—"

The light in the hallway was too dim to see clearly, but I could practically feel Mom frowning. "It's nothing. Just . . . just, good night, Mom."

The words seemed to hang there in the hallway. Then Mom turned away. "One month, Izzy," she called, heading into the kitchen. "And then we're going home."

CHAPTER 21

The next day, Dex wasn't on the bus, but Romy and Anderson were. As soon as Romy saw me, she grinned and waved me over.

"Hey," I said, finding my seat. "What are you doing here?" Anderson didn't usually ride our bus since he had his own car.

He slumped in his seat, a little sheepish. "My parents may have gotten their credit card bill this month, and they may have discovered that I used their American Express to buy some stuff for PMS."

"Check it," Romy said, nudging Anderson. He opened his backpack, and I could make out some black plastic device that I guessed was his EVP recorder. "I'm totally going to pay them back," Anderson said, zipping up his bag. "But it was on sale, so it made sense to go ahead and buy it, you know?"

"Absolutely," Romy agreed. "But it sucks that they took your car away."

Anderson shrugged. "Just for a few weeks. And hey, it means I get to hang out with you guys more."

I was apparently included in the "you guys," but you wouldn't have known that from the way Anderson's gaze lingered on Romy.

Covering a smile, I asked, "So where's Dex this morning?"

"He texted me that he was running late," Anderson offered, lifting his legs to prop his feet on my seat. As he did, his leg brushed Romy's, and I saw her give a little jump.

She cleared her throat, twisting her ponytail around one finger. "Did he say why?"

Anderson rolled his eyes. "You know Dex. He said it was because his Nana needed him to deliver a covert message to a Colombian drug runner, but he'd be in by lunch."

I snorted with laughter, but Romy frowned. "I bet it was another asthma attack. He's been getting them more often lately."

"Is it bad?" I asked. "His asthma?"

Romy and Anderson nodded in unison. "He laughs it off, but yeah," Anderson said. "It can be scary."

The image of Dex gasping for breath suddenly flashed in my brain, and I felt my chest tighten. *A job, a job, a job,* I repeated in my head.

"He hasn't lived here long, has he?"

Romy shook her head. "Just since August." And then suddenly she turned to Anderson and said, "Okay, you need to go away for a second."

His sneakers, which had been resting on the back of my seat, thudded to the floor. "Why?"

"Because Izzy and I need to talk girl stuff, and you can't be a part of that."

I don't know if Anderson was just used to following Romy's orders, or if he was terrified we'd start talking about Tampax, but in any case, he moved pretty quickly a few rows away. Reaching over the seat, Romy tugged my hand. "Come here."

Moving over to the now-vacant seat beside her, I raised my eyebrows. "What is it? Something about PMS? I mean, the ghost-hunting PMS, not the . . . regular kind. Unless you want to talk about that, because we can."

Romy waved her hand. "No, no business and not that kind of girl stuff. The more fun kind of girl stuff." She leaned closer, her dark eyes sparkling. "Do you like Dex?"

She'd whispered it, but I still looked around, hoping

no one had overheard. "First off, shhhh! And . . . yeah, of course I do. I like all of you."

"No, but I mean do you *like* him? You know, in the carnal sense."

I rolled my eyes. "You've clearly been spending too much time with Dex."

Romy smiled and poked me in the middle of my chest with one lime-green fingernail. "And so have you, if what my sources at the Dairee Kween tell me is correct. Were you two on a date there last night?"

"Please," I hissed. "The shushing. Could you at least try? And no, we weren't on a date. We were just . . . hanging out."

"In the sexy way."

There it was again. That giggle. That sound I supposedly didn't make. "No," I whispered, trying to look stern. "In the *friendly* way."

"Mmm-hmm," Romy said, narrowing her eyes.

"What about you?" I said, ducking my head closer. "I saw you jump when Anderson's leg brushed yours."

Now it was her turn to hiss, "Shhhhh!"

Smiling, I leaned back in my seat. "Ah, I see. It's different when the shoe is on the other foot."

"There are no shoes on any feet," Romy insisted, but the tips of her ears had gone pink. "Anderson and I are just friends."

"So we're just two awesome, ghost-hunting girls with two boys who may be cute, but are most definitely nothing more than friends," I said, and Romy grinned.

"We are. Which is why I'm going to share this with you, even though I was going to hog it all to myself for the ride."

With that, she reached into her backpack. I don't know what I expected her to pull out. A tinfoil hat, maybe. A pamphlet on twenty-first-century ghost-hunting techniques.

Instead, she whipped out a glossy issue of *Rockin' Grrls!* magazine, complete with articles like, "What His Dog Says About His Kissing Style!" and "Is It Wrong to Be in Love with Your Stepbrother?"

"Perfect," I said.

Romy and I spent the rest of the bus ride reading *Rockin' Grrls!*, and then I spent the walk to class telling her all about *Ivy Springs*.

"So this Leslie chick works at a circus?" Romy asked as we slid into English.

"Not, like, all the time. Only since her mom married a trapeze artist."

Romy stared at me. "Okay, I clearly need to see this show immediately. You said you own it?"

When I nodded, Romy pointed at me. "Then you are

going to bring it to my house next week, and we're going to watch all of it."

"There are over sixty episodes," I told her, raising my voice a little to be heard over the third bell.

"Make it next Friday, then. You can spend the night, and we'll do a whole marathon."

"Awesome," I said, and was surprised to find that I really meant it. And not so that I could ask her more about Dex, or try to find out what she knew about supernatural stuff. Just because hanging out with Romy and watching Leslie and Everton fight/make out/break up/get engaged for a few days sounded like . . . fun. Lots of it, actually.

Mrs. Steele announced that we'd be doing group work this morning, so we all started moving our desks, forming little circles. Apparently we'd been paired up based on who sat closest to us, so in addition to Romy, our group included Adam.

Ugh.

I braced myself for the awkward, and Adam more than delivered. Barely looking at me, he opened his binder and leaned as far away as he could.

Another desk bumped mine, and I glanced up to see Beth, Ben McCrary's girlfriend. I expected her to give me the cold shoulder, what with my dislocating her *boy-friend's* shoulder, but she didn't even seem to know who

I was. In fact, as we got to work on the assignment—answering a series of discussion questions about *Macbeth*—Beth didn't pay attention to any of us. Her eyes were far off, distracted, and when Romy asked her to copy down question four, Beth blinked at her like she wasn't even speaking English.

"What?"

"Question four?" Romy repeated, lifting her eyebrows. "'How does the supernatural influence Macbeth's actions?'"

Beth just shook her head. "I . . . I don't know." She gave a little shiver and crossed her arms tightly over her chest. "And can we please skip the questions about the supernatural?"

Romy glanced at me. "That's, like, half the questions."

"Lotta ghosts in *Macbeth*," I offered, tapping my pen against my paper. Beth looked me, huge dark circles under her eyes. She blinked twice before turning back to Romy.

"You do that ghost-hunting club, right?"

On my other side, Adam snorted but didn't say anything. Romy flashed him a quick glare.

"Yeah," she told Beth. "Why?"

Beth swallowed, her throat working convulsively. "Have you ever seen a ghost?"

Now Adam folded his arms, entire body radiating disdain, but neither Romy nor I paid him any attention.

"Not seen, exactly," Romy said, her eyes practically glowing as she moved closer to Beth. "But sensed, sure. I can show you all kind of notes on ghostly activity in—"

"I saw a ghost in my house," Beth blurted out. Then she swung her head from one side to the other, making sure no one could overhear. Her blond hair hung limply around her shoulders, and when she laid both hands on her desk, I saw that they were trembling. "I mean . . . I think I did. For the past few nights, I've heard these weird sounds outside my room, like someone was walking down the hall. But when I got up, th-there was no one. And I thought I was just hearing things, but then last night—" She broke off, chewing her lip. Romy had her fingers curled around the edge of her desk, and even Adam seemed interested now. There was no disguising the real terror in Beth's voice. "I woke up, and there was this . . . this shape standing by my bed. All glowing and hazy, and I tried to yell, but it was like my throat wasn't working, and then it just . . . it just vanished."

Romy was practically vibrating with excitement, but I frowned. Last night? I'd sealed Mary Evans in her grave last night. There was no way she could be floating around Beth Tanner's house.

Beth caught my expression. "You don't believe me," she said flatly.

"No," I said, shaking my head. "It's not that, it's just—"

"Maybe you were dreaming," Adam suggested, and Beth's lower lip wobbled.

"I wasn't . . . You know what? Just forget it. It was stupid anyway." With that, she slammed her notebook shut and got up, asking Mrs. Steele if she could go to the restroom.

As she left, Adam folded his arms on top of his desk, leaning toward me. "Do you think it's drugs? I bet it's drugs. I took an awareness course about drugs last year. At the *community college*."

I was still staring at the door, so it took me a moment to realize Adam was looking at me.

"Huh?"

"Beth Tanner. On drugs. Is she? Because I'm voting yes."

"Don't be a jerk, Adam," Romy snapped. "She was really freaked out." Twisting in her desk, Romy faced me. "We should talk to her. When she gets back. Maybe PMS could go over to her house, see if we can pick up any energy readings—"

"You have got to be kidding me," Adam groaned, and Romy turned back around.

"You should take this more seriously," she said. "Look at what happened to Mr. Snyder, and now Beth. You could be next."

I knew Romy was doing that thing she did a lot—assuming everyone knew exactly what she was thinking. But Adam didn't know about the picture of him with Beth and Mr. Snyder, or Romy's theory that Mary was seeking revenge on the founding families of Ideal, so he just stared at her, eyes wide.

"Um . . . what the hell does that mean?"

Romy's face was bright red, but the bell rang, saving her from having to answer. Adam shoved his desk back and began gathering his things, muttering something about "freaks" under his breath.

As Romy and I headed for the door, she turned to me. "It had to be Mary that Beth saw, right? Which means her spirit isn't just tied to the school."

I just nodded, lost in thought. It *couldn't* be Mary. I knew how to deal with ghosts, and the salt thing had never failed. Was there another ghost prowling the halls of the school?

I saw Beth one more time, during P.E., but she just sat on the bleachers, surrounded by her friends and still looking kind of gray. I tried to catch her eye, hoping to talk to her a little more about what she'd seen, but every time our eyes met, she looked away.

By the end of the day, I'd nearly convinced myself that Beth was wrong. The doll had unsettled her, and who could blame her? A mutilated Barbie that looks like you strung up in your locker? That would upset anyone. Still, worry slithered through me. This was supposed to be a simple, easy job. I couldn't have screwed *this* up, too.

Romy and Dex were both waiting for me by my locker when the last bell rang, and if a little thrill ran through me at seeing Dex standing there, seemingly okay, I tried my best to ignore it. He had his shoulder against the door, leaning down to listen to Romy. As I got closer, I could hear her saying, "Maybe Mary has some sort of grudge against those families."

"So the ghost of Mary Evans is pissed off at the descendants of *some* people who did some*thing*. For some *reason*," Dex summed up. When Romy nodded, he bent down, taking her shoulder. "Rome, can you hear yourself when you talk?"

Irritated, Romy rolled her shoulder, knocking Dex's hand off. "Why are you even in PMS if you don't believe in this kind of stuff?"

"Because this school is so boring, I thought I might actually die, and ghost hunting seemed like a fun way to spend some time," he replied. "And it is fun. I like creeping around abandoned buildings, and scouring cemeteries, and pouring salt on— Oof!" He grunted as my elbow slammed into his ribs.

Looking down at me, Dex made a face, but added, "Fries. I like pouring salt on fries after I've creeped around abandoned buildings and scoured cemeteries. It's just . . . this seems like a stretch, Romy."

Romy pressed her lips together, and I wasn't sure if she was hurt or angry. Finally, she spit out "Whatever" and stormed away from us. I stood there, torn. Dex and Romy were both my friends, but now they were mad at each other. Was I breaking some kind of girl code by *not* walking away with Romy?

"Rome!" Dex called after her. She didn't turn around but she did raise her hand and flip him off.

Dex just sighed. "Well, that'll be with us for a while. Romy can hold a grudge like no one's business."

"You shouldn't have picked on her," I told him as I put my things in my backpack.

"I didn't!" he cried. "I just pointed out that her theory is insane."

"Which she saw as picking on her," I said once we'd joined the flow of students heading toward the parking lot. The buses lined up under an awning.

"Okay, so maybe I could have phrased it a little nicer, but life at Mary Evans High is rough enough for Romy. The PMS thing has already made her a target. If she starts spouting off about a ghost wanting to kill the home-coming queen . . ." He shook his head. "There would be no end to the crap they'd give her."

"So you were trying to protect her by . . . being mean to her?"

By now we were outside. While the other, luckier kids who had their own cars walked through the parking lot, Dex and I took our places on the sidewalk. Romy was several feet away, very pointedly not looking at us.

"I just know how tough it can be when everyone thinks you're some kind of freak," Dex said, his voice suddenly tight. "When I was a kid—"

He broke off, staring somewhere beyond my shoulder. "What the hell?"

I turned, catching a sudden movement out of the corner of my eye. A car down at the far end of the parking lot was driving toward us. And it was going . . . fast. Way too fast considering the fact that kids were walking out to their cars. One of those kids passed me, and I realized it was Beth.

She froze, staring down the parking lot at the car. "Oh my God," I heard her mutter. And then the car was moving faster, and it seemed to dawn on me and Beth at the same time that it was headed for her.

And that no one was behind the wheel.

I didn't think. I launched myself toward Beth,

shoving someone out of my way. I heard a pained cry, but by then I was already to Beth. The two of us went stumbling into a parked car, my elbow smacking the side-view mirror so hard I bit my lip. Beth crumpled to the ground between two cars as I fell nearly on top of her.

Just behind us, I could hear the squeal of rubber, the sick crunch of metal on metal. And shrieking. There was a lot of shrieking.

"Are you okay?" I asked Beth, which was probably a stupid question seeing as how she was pale and sobbing. "What happened?" she kept asking. "What was that?"

It was a really good question.

I stood up and took in the chaos raging around me. The car had plowed right into one of the parked buses. Luckily, no one had been on it, and all the kids waiting to board seemed to have gotten out of the way.

A flash of movement caught my eye, and I turned back to Beth's car. There, sitting in driver's seat, was the spirit of Mary Evans. She was a lot fainter than she'd been the night of the basketball game, and no one else seemed to see the ghost, but there was no doubt in my mind that's who she was.

In a flash, she was gone, and I could almost convince myself that it had been a trick of the light.

I had laid salt all over that grave. It wasn't possible for her to be out and wreaking havoc.

Unless I'd screwed up somehow. But it was spreading salt. How hard was that?

But Dex had been there that night. Could he have done something that made the banishing not take? I scanned the crowd for Romy and Dex, finally finding them back on the sidewalk, near the school. I made my way toward them, stepping over Ben McCrary. He was lying on the grass, clutching his shoulder. Apparently he was who I'd shoved. Oops. "Um . . . sorry," I said, but he made a shrieky sound and scuttled farther away from me.

"Are you guys okay?" I asked once I'd reached Romy and Dex.

"Us?" Romy asked, pushing her hair out of her face. "You're the one who just leapt on Beth Tanner like a ninja."

"Yeah," Dex added. "That was . . . if I say hot, does that make me a perv?"

In spite of all the adrenaline coursing through me—or maybe because of it—I started laughing. And once I'd started, Dex joined in, and then Romy was laughing, too. The three of us stood there for a long time, cracking up while everyone around us looked horrified.

But when I turned back to the bus, my laughter died in my throat. Two teachers were helping Beth up from the ground. Coach Lewis was there, too, gesturing at the crowd. "Back up, back up!" By now, a siren was wailing in the distance, and a group was starting to form around the wrecked car.

"Wow," Dex said softly, as though the seriousness of what had happened was just starting to sink in. "She really could have been hurt."

I watched him carefully. None of this made sense. If Dex had screwed up the banishing on purpose, he was the best actor in the world. He looked genuinely freaked out right now.

"She could have *died*," Romy said, and then she closed a hand around my wrist. "But you saved her."

I tried to smile back and not think that if I'd done my job right, she wouldn't have needed saving at all.

CHAPTER 22

"I used enough salt," I told Torin later that evening. We'd just watched three episodes of *Ivy Springs*, but I hadn't concentrated on any of them. I'd been too busy going over everything that had happened that afternoon. "I know I did. But it didn't lock Mary in."

Torin scratched his chin. "That's exceedingly unusual."

I know Mom had said to stop going to Torin for advice, but, well, he was here and she wasn't. And this was definitely a day that required advice. Lots of it.

"It's more than just that; it's impossible," I replied, flipping onto my back to gaze at the ceiling. Whoever had lived here before us had put up a bunch of those plastic stars. "Ghosts can't fight the salt thing. It's part of why they're so un-fun to hunt."

Torin was quiet for a moment before saying, "You said both the teacher and the student received little . . . gifts. Warnings of their impending fate."

"Yup. A squashed frog and a jacked-up Barbie."

"That's smart," Torin said. "Fear makes spirits stronger. It's why older hauntings are so hard to dispose of. The longer a spirit can build up and live off of fear, the more powerful it is."

I turned over, facing Torin. "I've never heard that before."

Torin crossed his arms, smug. "Oh, how I love knowing things you don't. It's such a satisfying feeling."

"Well, now I *do* know it, so thanks for that."

"Hmm," Torin acknowledged with a nod. "That is the price for sharing my wisdom."

With a huge sigh, Torin flopped down onto my bed in the mirror. Looking at the reflection, it was like we were lying side by side. "So the ghost is strong because of fear," I said, dangling my legs off the bed. "But . . . ghosts are pretty much always scary. Why go the extra mile?"

"There's a difference between fear and terror," Torin said. "Terror is a much stronger emotion. It feeds all sorts of negative energy. Appearing in her ghostly form to these people would have, to use your vernacular, freaked them out. But leaving little gifts telling them how they'd be attacked? That builds a sort of anticipatory terror. Like fuel for a ghost. And when you have a ghost that's already terribly strong due to being summoned by magic, well. You end up with a problem like this on your hands."

I mulled that over. "But why summon a ghost?"

Torin was uncharacteristically silent, and when I tilted my head to look at him, he was fiddling with his cuff. "Torin?" I prompted.

"Spirits are not always summoned on purpose," he said at last. "There are times, if one is doing a particularly advanced spell, for instance, that the magic can have . . . unintended consequences. If, for example, one was attempting to raise the dead—"

"You can't do that. It's not possible to bring somebody back to life."

Sniffing prissily, Torin dropped his sleeve. "Of course. I'm sure your vast amounts of knowledge amassed over the past sixteen years greatly outweigh my own centuries-long existence and personal experiences."

Torin tended to get extra-flowery when his feelings were hurt, and I sat up, moving a little closer to his mirror. "I'm sorry," I said, meaning it. "It's just . . . Wait, have you raised the dead?"

"I'm not saying that," Torin replied, but he didn't quite meet my eyes. "I'm only saying that if you have a ghost who is resistant to salt, you probably have a witch as well, and one attempting seriously dark magic at that."

Chewing on my lower lip, I thought about Dex. He'd been there the night I'd tried to seal Mary into her grave, and it hadn't worked.

"You have that expression on your face that speaks of incipient moral dubiousness," Torin observed, making me glad I'd bought that thesaurus a few years back.

"Yeah, I'm about to get super morally dubious, Torin. Remember the other day, when you asked if I wanted you to go in Dex's mirror?"

"I do," he said, narrowing his eyes.

"And remember how I said I didn't want you to?"

"Indeed."

"I take it back." It was awful, I knew that. No matter what Dex was, he was my friend, and using my magic mirror to spy on him was most definitely Not Okay. But people were getting hurt, so I couldn't afford to be a good person right now. And somewhere deep inside, I must've know this was going to happen. Otherwise, why had I studied his mailbox number when he'd driven me past his house the other night?

I gave the address to Torin, telling myself that this was the only way. Being a Brannick meant making hard choices. Mom had once said it meant choosing what was right over what our hearts wanted. I thought she might have been talking about my dad, but I hadn't had the courage to ask.

Still, when Torin gave me a flourishing salute and vanished, I had to swallow the urge to call him back, tell him to forget it. But it was too *late*.

Sighing, I turned to my TV, hoping Everton and Leslie's problems could distract me from my own. I was only about five minutes in when there was a soft knock at my door. Even though I knew Torin was long gone, I shot a glance at the mirror before calling, "Come in!"

Mom opened the door and leaned against the jamb. "There was a car accident at your school today," she said without preamble. "Anything to do with you?"

"Kind of?"

Mom took that in. "Anything I need to know about?"

I glanced at my mirror. "No," I said at last. "I got this."

Mom took a deep breath through her nose, but in the end, she just nodded. "Okay. Anything more on that boy?"

I tried hard to keep my eyes off the mirror this time. "He invited me to his house to meet his grandmother. Figured I'd take him up on that, see if there are any clues."

"Good idea," Mom replied with a little nod. "Have you finished your homework?"

"Yes." We'd had lots of extra time to wait while they

towed the car and the dented bus, and I'd tackled the rest of my *Macbeth* questions as well as the first few paragraphs of my essay. Dex and Romy, thankfully, had made up. When a new bus had finally arrived, they were joking and teasing each other again.

"Okay," Mom said slowly. When I glanced up, she was still hovering in the doorway.

"I thought we might go out to dinner tonight."

"Does this town have restaurants?" I asked. "I mean, other than the Dairee Kween?"

Mom gave a snort that sounded close to laughter. "I passed that place today. I don't think I can trust anywhere that mangles the English language like that."

"I think I saw a Chinese place next to Walmart." I said. "I could go for some lo mein."

"Chinese it is," said Mom, pushing off of the jamb. "Meet me downstairs in ten."

The drive to the restaurant was quiet, but in a nice way. We didn't mention the case during dinner. Instead we talked about school, and I told her about Romy and PMS and one of the articles I'd read on the bus: "Twenty Uses for Your Hair Dryer You've Never Thought Of!" Mom didn't talk much, but she listened, and I decided that was good enough.

Once we were done and Mom had paid the bill, I figured we'd head home. I was kind of anxious to see if

Torin was back yet. But instead, Mom started the car and said, "Why don't we drive around for a bit?"

"Um . . . sure."

If the drive over to the restaurant had been pleasant, this one was just . . . weird. When I flipped on the radio, Mom immediately reached out and turned it off. And she kept leaning over the steering wheel and peering out into the darkness, cocking her head like she was listening for something.

But it wasn't until she pulled in front of a house and shut off the ignition that I finally got what was going on.

"A job?"

She shrugged. "Maybe. The other day I was having breakfast at the Waffle Hut, and these two guys there seemed shady, so—"

I rolled my eyes. "Mom, everyone at the Waffle Hut is shady. That's why they go to the Waffle Hut. To . . . be shady. And eat waffles. Shadily."

Mom sat back in her seat. "I just . . . I needed to do something."

"Something other than your research?" I asked, and Mom's sigh seemed to come up from the soles of her feet.

"Why won't you tell me what you're looking into?" I asked, and to my horror, my voice came out thin and high, like I was on the verge of tears. "If it's about . . .

about Finley, at least let me try to help. I know I messed up that night, but I wouldn't—"

She turned to me, and once again I was struck by how much she looked like Finn. All high cheekbones and pouty lips and strong jaw. "What happened to Finley was not your fault, Isolde," she said, using that commanding tone again. "I don't think that, and I never want you to think it, either."

I tugged at the drawstring of my hoodie. "I miss her a lot."

A car drove past us, and it must have been a trick of the light, because I could've sworn Mom's lower lip trembled a little. "I know you do."

It wasn't, "me, too," but at least it was something.

Leaning back, I thumped my head against my seat. "We're not going to find her, are we?"

Mom was quiet for so long that I wondered if she would even answer. And then she said, "I don't know."

Something about being in the dark in the car made all of it easier to say. "What are we going to do? If we *don't* find her. We're the last two Brannicks in the world. Do we just keep hunting monsters even though it's crazy dangerous? Until there are no Brannicks left?"

A muscle worked in Mom's jaw, but she didn't answer. For a long time, the only sound was the ticking of the cooling engine. Then, sounding as tired as I felt,

Mom said, "I don't know, Isolde. All I know to do is . . . this." She nodded toward the house, but I knew she didn't mean this specific job. "My mother died in the field. So did my cousins and aunts and nearly every Brannick I have ever known. But I don't know what to do with myself if I'm not doing this. And searching through ancient, useless books for some clue as to what happened to Finn . . . I just feel like I'm going crazy. Following those guys from the Waffle Hut, thinking they might be Prodigium, was the first time I've felt happy in weeks."

I turned to stare at her. "Mom. That is . . . deeply effed up."

She gave a harsh bark of laughter, but there was no humor in it. "That's being a Brannick, Izzy. Now come on. Let's get home."

We didn't say anything else the whole way home, both of us lost in our own thoughts.

Back in my room, I searched the mirror, but Torin was still gone. I didn't know if that was good or bad.

I shucked my clothes, got my pajamas on, and spent the next few hours on my computer searching for anything to do with Mary Evans and ghost summoning. Mom was right: this is what Brannicks do. We hunt monsters, we save people, we keep our eyes on the ball. I had let myself get too distracted with Dex and Romy and

Macbeth essays. . . . It was time to solve this case and get out of Ideal. Time to let Mom get back on a case, too, rather than just following some possibly creepy dudes at the Waffle Hut.

When Mom knocked on my door and called, "Lights out," I knew what my next step would be.

I closed the laptop and got into bed, thinking I was too keyed up to sleep. But I must have dozed off at some point, because the next think I knew, Torin was there, whispering, "Isolde."

I sat up, afraid that I was in another one of my Torin-created dreams. But no, there he was, standing in my mirror. "Torin?" My voice was thick with sleep.

"If your lad is up to mischief, he wasn't indulging tonight," Torin said, and I was shocked by the wave of relief that flooded through me. "Nothing supernatural about him except just how many hours he can play video games," Torin added, giving a massive yawn.

"Good," I told him. "And thanks."

In the glass, he seemed to be sitting in my desk chair, leaning back with his arms folded behind his head. "Is that it, then? Are we done?"

I rolled back over in bed, looking out my window. "No," I said softly. "We're just beginning."

CHAPTER 23

"Okay, so if everyone will just look at their handout, we can get started."

Romy, Dex, and Anderson watched me with varying degree of "WTF?" stamped on their faces as I stood at the front of the portable classroom, dry-erase marker clutched in my hand. I'd called an emergency meeting of PMS that morning before class, so we didn't have much time before the bell rang. The sooner I got them on board with this idea, the sooner we could stop Mary.

"When did you have time to make handouts?" Dex finally asked.

"That's not important. The important part is high-lighted halfway down on page two."

There was a rustling of papers as they all flipped to that section. "This . . . this says 'On Witches, Ghosts, and

Summonings.'" Anderson stared at me with wide dark eyes. "Summonings? Are we dealing with, like, exorcist-level stuff here?"

"Not exactly." I turned back to the whiteboard and began writing. "Okay, so Mary Evans's ghost was summoned by a witch. I'm not sure why, but that doesn't matter so much right now. The main thing is to find out *who* raised her."

Behind me, I heard Dex say, "Um, Professor Brannick, I have questions. And they are legion."

"I'll take questions at the end."

"I was joking," Dex murmured, but I was on a roll. "So, ghost summoning is not that hard if you know where to do it. And there are two places where a witch could've summoned Mary Evans. One, the place where she's buried, and two, the place where she died."

I turned to face the other members of PMS. "Now, we know where Mary is buried, and according to the legend, she died in the cave where she used to meet her teacher. If you'll flip to page three, you'll see I've attached a map of where I think this cave probably is. Tomorrow night, we're going to split up and go to those places. Dex and Anderson, you take the grave; me and Romy will take the cave." I paused. "Hey, that rhymes. Anyway, once we figure out who raised Mary's ghost, we can figure out why, and we can stop it. And now I'll take questions."

Three hands went up.

I called on Dex first. "Um, yes. We have this friend, Izzy Brannick? She's about your height, has your color hair, and she is a normal, sane-type person. And you, Crazy Lady, seem to have replaced her. Can we have Izzy back now please?"

Rolling my eyes, I pointed at Romy. "Next."

"Actually, I kind of want you to answer Dex's question. Seriously, Izzy. What is going on with you?"

"Just trying to be a . . . a productive member of PMS. So are we all agreed? Friday night, the boys deal with the cemetery, the girls handle the cave."

"Um," Anderson said, flicking his hair out of his eyes, "I, uh, was wondering if I could be paired up with Romy instead. No offense, Dex, it's just . . ."

Dex held up a hand. "None taken." Then he gave an exaggerated leer. "I'd much rather spelunk with Izzy, anyway."

I knew that spelunking meant exploring caves, but I glared at Dex like he'd said something inappropriate.

"Now see, there's the Izzy I know," he teased, and I suddenly found myself smiling back. Ugh. I was clearly losing it.

Shaking my head, I rattled my own handouts. "Okay, so me and Dex take the cave; Romy and Anderson, you're on grave duty. We'll be looking for anything that suggests a ritual has taken place. Candles, burn marks, funky smells . . ."

"Salt all over the grass," Dex said under his breath, but neither Romy nor Anderson paid him any attention.

"So . . . witches," Romy said, frowning at the paper.

"Yes. Well, witch, singular at least."

She looked up at me, squinting behind her glasses. "Pointy-hat-wearing, broomstick-riding witches."

"They don't actually do any of that stuff. At least most of them don't. Some of them like to be retro every once and a while."

Anderson lifted an eyebrow. "And you know this because?"

I glanced over at Dex. "I read a lot. On the Internet. And also I went to this fancy all-girls' school, and we had a whole class on . . . witches."

When the three of them just continued to stare at me, I added, "It was a really progressive school. Anyway, tonight, PMS patrol, cool?"

"I don't have anything better to do tonight," Anderson said, draping his arm around the back of Romy's chair.

Her dimples deepened as she tried to hide a smile. "Me neither," she said.

"You know I'm always up for weirdness my Nana won't approve of," Dex said, clapping his hands together. "Speaking of, since you'll have to ride with me tonight,

Izzy, why don't we get off the bus together this afternoon? You can meet my Nana."

"Right," I said. I'd been meaning to do that, and while I wish I'd found time to see if any of those magazines had articles like, "Meeting His Nana: What Does It Mean?" there was no time like the present. "That . . . yeah, sure, that'll be fine."

Dex leaned forward, his blue eyes bright. "So let's do this. PMS's first witch hunt!"

The bell rang, and the four of us hurried to gather up our stuff and get back into the main building. The boys loped off ahead while Romy and I hung back a little.

"Anderson was in that picture," she said, worrying her thumbnail between her teeth. "If I'm right, and Mary's after the descendants of certain people—"

"There were lots of people in that picture, Romy," I said, looping my arm through hers. I still hadn't found the appropriate time to do a hip bump, but arm-looping felt right. "And Anderson is going to be fine because we're going to find out what's causing the haunting and put a stop to it. Besides, Mary's nice enough to leave us little warnings when she picks a victim. If anything freaky happens to Anderson, he'll tell us, and we'll know."

That didn't seem to make Romy feel better, so I tightened my arm in hers. "Or hey! Maybe she's done with the whole revenge thing. Maybe it was just Snyder's and Beth's relatives she was pissed at."

That theory lasted until second period. Just after P.E., Romy and I were standing by her locker when there was suddenly an explosive *bang* from farther down the hallway.

"The hell?" I heard someone squawk as a cloud of gray smoke began pouring out of a locker.

"Anderson?" Romy cried, but it wasn't Anderson standing in front of the Exploding Locker. It was Adam, his face a mask of fear and annoyance.

Rushing down the hall, I grabbed his arm. "Are you okay?"

Irritated, he threw off my hand. "Yeah, fine. Just some jackass put a firecracker or something in my locker." Waving the smoke away, he peered inside, and I leaned over his shoulder to do the same. All that was left of Adam's textbooks was a smoldering pile of ash.

"All right, people, make a hole," Mrs. Steele said, pushing students out of her way. Grimacing, she took in the mess. "First someone's car malfunctions, now lockers are exploding? What has gotten *into* this place?"

Behind her back, my eyes met Romy's. Apparently, Mary was far from done.

CHAPTER 24

"Okay, please do not be alarmed by our yard situation," Dex said as I followed him up the driveway. "Nana is a fearsome cook but a truly dreadful gardener. It is known."

Dex exaggerated about a lot of things, but the state of his yard was not one of them. Even though it was late February and nothing was exactly blooming, every bush and blade of grass in Dex's front yard was brown and crispy-looking. Even the pear tree looked in danger of keeling over.

But the house itself was pretty. Nicer than ours and a little bigger, there were cheerful yellow curtains in the windows, and when Dex opened the front door, I froze and took a deep breath.

I don't know what heaven smells like, but if it doesn't

smell like freshly baked cookies, I will be really disappointed.

Seeing my rapturous expression, Dex grinned. "This way," he said, tugging me into the kitchen.

A woman in a light blue sweater and a pair of what I'm pretty sure could be described as Mom Jeans—Nana Jeans?—was pulling a tray of cookies out of the oven as we walked in.

"Dex!" she cried happily. And then her eyes swung to me. They were the same bright blue as Dex's, and they nearly matched her sweater. "And who is this?"

"Izzy, my Nana, Nana, my Izzy."

I shot Dex a glare as his Nana put the tray of cookies on the counter. "Oh, my!" she exclaimed, flapping her hands. "Dexter, if you're going to have company, especially such lovely company, you need to warn your Nana! I look a *mess*."

She actually looked pretty nice, in my opinion. Her hair, like Dex's, was black and curly, with only a few touches of gray at her temples. Glasses perched on the edge of her nose, fastened to a sparkly chain draped around her neck. As she reached out and enfolded me in a hug, I caught a whiff of vanilla and baby powder.

Basically, Dex's Nana was the Perfect Grandmother. When she pulled away, she even patted my cheek. "Oh, aren't you a pretty thing. Dex said you were, but it's nice to see he didn't exaggerate for once."

My cheeks flamed at that, and next to me, Dex nudged my ribs. "If anything, I undersold her, didn't I, Nana?"

She swatted at his arm. "Now, Dexter, you're making her blush. Come on and grab a couple of cookies, and tell me all about yourself, Izzy. What a sweet name. Is that short for Isabelle?"

"Isolde," I told her, scooping up a cookie from the tray. Dex sat down on a gingham-covered stool and patted the one next to him. I sat, taking a bit of my cookie. It was everything I had hoped it would be and more. I wondered if Dex's Nana would consider adopting me.

"How pretty," she said. She moved to the giant stainless steel fridge and pulled out a carton of milk. "Wasn't there a famous story about an Isolde? Something beautiful and tragic?"

"Tristan and Isolde," Dex said before I could answer. "And quite frankly, I'm hoping the romance of Dexter and Isolde ends up with a lower body count."

Nana tittered, and I brushed stray crumbs of cookie from my mouth. "There is not a romance of Dexter and Isolde," I said, but I caught myself smiling anyway. Then I remembered. Dex was not just some boy, and I was not just some girl sitting in his Nana's kitchen, eating the most wonderful cookies ever created by woman. He was some kind of Prodigium, and I was here to find out what.

And even if there hadn't been that, romance between me and Dex was totally out of the question. I tried to imagine taking him home to Mom, introducing him as my boyfriend. Brannick women were always very careful about the men they chose. They had the bloodline to think about, after all, which was why they tended to pick warriors. Soldiers, Navy SEALS. My grandfather had even been a Green Beret.

Whenever Mom had talked about Finley's and my dad, the one word that always came up was "strong." Dex couldn't even jog around the football field without his asthma flaring up.

And it wasn't just that. How would Mom react to a boy who was so purely . . . decorative? Sure, Dex had salted a grave, but he'd taken his nice coat off first.

I shook those thoughts off. They were unproductive and pointless. Instead, I smiled at Nana and said, "So you and Dex moved here from New York?" I thought as far as questions went, it was fairly harmless. But I didn't miss the way Nana stiffened slightly. "We've lived a little bit of everywhere. And I've told Dex that the important thing is the future, not the past."

She stroked his hair. "He's here now, and that's all that matters."

Dex smiled at her, but there was something kind of puzzled about it. Maybe he thought her answer was as weird as I did, but it almost seemed like more than that. It was the same look Finn used to get when she couldn't remember where she'd put her crossbow. (That happened a lot more often than it should have, if you asked me. You should always know where you've left deadly weapons.)

"Nana's right," Dex finally said, slapping a hand on the counter. "As Shakespeare said, 'Don't look back, you should never look back.'"

"That was a Don Henley song, dear, but it's an excellent sentiment nonetheless," Nana said, patting his hand. Weirdness passed, she smiled at me again. "Izzy, will you be staying for dinner?"

If the rest of her food was as good as her cookies, I'd be an idiot not to.

Dex answered for me. "She will be. And then we're going to go out for a while, if that's okay with you.

Nana's face creased into a frown. "Are you sure that's a good idea, sweetie? Your asthma has been so bad lately—"

But Dex just waved that off. "I'm fine. It's the time of year or something. Asthma season. But I have my trusty inhaler"—he pulled it out of his coat pocket, shaking it— "and the Fair Isolde to protect me if need be."

When Nana didn't stop frowning, Dex dropped the act, leaning in closer to her. "I'll be fine, Nana," he said, his voice softer. He laid a hand over hers, and his bracelet caught the light. "You worry too much."

She touched the silver links around his wrist. "I'm your grandmother," she said. "It's allowed."

Watching them together made me smile, and started this kind of warm, blooming feeling in my chest. Not only was Dex cute and smart and funny, but he loved his Nana—

And that's when something occurred to me. Dex's Nana. She was related to him by blood. That meant if he was Prodigium, then so was she. That's how that worked; there was no skipping generations, no freak human kid born to Prodigium parents.

There were no vibes coming off of Nana, and she'd hugged me. Touched my cheek. I hadn't felt anything. Not even the slightest hint that she was Prodigium. Still, just to be sure, I leaned forward and said, "That's a pretty ring."

Just as I'd hoped, she pushed her hand toward me so that I could get a better look. As she did, I caught her fingers.

Nothing. Not even the slightest tingle.

"Thank you, sweetheart," she said. "I got it from one of those home-shopping shows. You know, the ones that come on late at night and make silly old ladies like me spend more than they should."

I laughed harder than necessary, trying to cover my confusion. Nana wasn't Prodigium, so Dex couldn't be one either. But if that was true, what the heck was I feeling? No matter what everyone kept saying, I knew that little hum of magic when I touched him wasn't just hormones.

I turned my head and looked at him grinning at his Nana, his silver bracelet winking in the sun, his coat just impossibly, stupidly purple.

Or did I just want Dex to be Prodigium because the idea of liking him was a lot scarier?

CHAPTER 25

Dex and I spent the rest of the afternoon playing video games. I'd never done that before, but it turned out all those years of training paid off in wicked hand-eye coordination. So while I couldn't beat Dex at Dragon Slayer IV, I didn't get totally embarrassed either. Once we'd slain dragons, we ate with Nana. Like her cookies, her spaghetti recipe clearly came from heaven, and by the time we left for the cave, I felt happier—and fuller—than I had in weeks.

Okay, so maybe Dex's Nana seemed a little overly protective. But Dex was her only grandkid and all the family she had. That was probably normal. And Dex was normal, I reminded myself as we drove to the outskirts of town. In the dim blue lights of the dash, I studied his profile. Normal. I'd never thought that word could sound so appealing.

The cave was easier to find than I'd thought it would be. There were signs and everything. Granted, they didn't mention Mary Evans or ghosts, but according to the legend, this had been where Mary and Jasper—the teacher—had met, and done . . . whatever. And, more important, where Mary had died.

Once we got there, Dex opened my door for me, holding out his hand. "Milady."

The night was cold enough that I wished I'd brought a heavier jacket. Dex was decked out in a new purple jacket, a thick green scarf knotted at his throat. He looked warm and cozy, and I wondered if his jacket was as soft as it seemed.

Dex must've picked up on my longing, because he went to unbutton his coat. "Cold? You can have it."

"No," I said quickly. "It's just . . . purple suits you. Which is good since you wear so much of it."

Preening, Dex raised his head and pushed his shoulders back. "It brings out the color of my eyes."

I didn't giggle this time, but I did give him a playful shove as I moved past him and into the cave. Once we were inside, we turned our flashlights on.

"Well, this is . . ."

"Creepy," I finished.

"I was actually going to go with 'pants-wettingly terrifying,' but, sure."

"You really think Mary and Jasper used this place to get all . . . romantic?" Running a hand over the damp walls of the cave, I shuddered a little. "Because seriously, I wouldn't even take my *hat* off in here."

"Their relationship was already pretty gross. Maybe they were going for some kind of grossness record."

"Lovely," I muttered, walking farther back into the cave. As I did, I had to crouch slightly. Dex had to practically fold in half. "Whoever used to hang out here, they must have been pretty tiny," I joked.

Dex turned his flashlight on me. "Um, Iz, pretty sure they weren't standing up," he said, and I blushed.

"Right," I said, trying to sound extra brusque so that he wouldn't notice my discomfort. "Okay, so. Proof of the supernatural. Let's find some."

Kneeling down, Dex yanked a melted candle off a little shelf carved in the rock. "You think this was supposed to be sexy or spooky?"

I was never going to stop blushing. I was actually going to die of blood loss because there wasn't any left to pump through my heart. It was all in my face.

"Nothing in this place is sexy," I told him, and he laughed.

"Oh, come on, Izzy. Even you, Miss Anti-Romance, can admit there's something just a little bit appealing about making out in a candlelit cave."

"Bats live in caves," I reminded him. "And where there are bats, there's bat poop. Lots of it. Did you know there's a cave in Mexico where they have a whole mountain made of guano?"

Dex leveled a fake-sultry gaze at me. "Are you coming on to me?"

I shined my flashlight at him, making him throw up a hand to guard his eyes. "Hey, watch it! You want me to actually see the ghost stuff, right?'

"Just . . . start looking, okay?"

"Fine," he grumbled, and we made our way deeper into the cave. The ceiling got lower and we both had to drop to our knees and crawl.

"Salting graves, crawling underground . . . you really are the most fun date ever," Dex mused. I bumped him with my shoulder and kept crawling. After a few feet, the cave opened up again, the ceiling soaring at least twelve feet overhead. Dex stood up and stretched with a happy groan, but all I could focus on was the magic bouncing off the rocks, filling the air, making my hair nearly stand on end. "This is it."

Frowning, Dex spun in a circle. "What, this? This is where the ghost stuff went down? How can you tell?"

"I just . . . can." It was maybe not the greatest answer ever, but I couldn't think of any other way to explain to Dex how I could sense magic.

Luckily, he didn't question it. "Whoa!" he cried.

"What?" Had he felt it? Was it just a delayed reaction? But Dex wasn't exclaiming over all the magic radiating inside the cave. He was walking forward to another little alcove carved in the rock.

"Aha," he said, poking around on the ground. "You're right, this is it."

I knelt next to him, turning my beam of light onto the cave floor. There was another melty candle and a few scraps of charred paper. Rooting around a little more, he uncovered a tiny golden charm. I leaned in closer as he laid it in his palm and shined the flashlight on it.

"A heart," he murmured.

I was suddenly aware that our heads were very close together, and took a deep breath. "Yeah."

His eyes dropped to my mouth. "That's both sexy and spooky, don't you think?"

"Depends on how you look at it, I guess," I said.

Now I was watching his mouth. Like his hands and eyes, Dex's lips were pretty. Beautiful, even. And suddenly I wanted them on mine more than I had ever wanted anything. Even as we moved closer together, some tiny part of my brain that was still a Brannick and not a silly girl losing her head over a cute boy registered what the magic in this cave must be. No ordinary spell had happened here. This was different. This was a love spell.

And now here Dex and I were, soaking in all this love spell energy. That was why he was staring at me like he wanted to devour me. Why I *wanted* him to devour me. It was residual energy from the spell, nothing else. I don't know how I did it, but I managed to get to my feet and back away from him.

Clearing my throat, I started shining my flashlight around the rest of the cave. "There might be more stuff. I mean, that's definitely magiclike, and—"

"I've never kissed anyone in a cave," Dex mused. When I turned around, he was still on his knees, watching me. "Or in any kind of underground structure, really. Cave, bomb shelter, secret government bunker . . ." His light was on me again. "What about you? You seem like the kind of girl whose romantic life is full of thrills and danger."

My "romantic life" consisted of watching cheesy teen soaps and sneaking the occasional drugstore romance novel, but wasn't the kind of thing I wanted to share.

And I definitely wasn't telling him that I'd never kissed anyone anywhere before. "Lots," I told him, going for breezy. "There was a secret tunnel connecting my school to the boys' school down the road. So it was all underground making out all the time."

"I knew it," he said, making me laugh. "So these boys you were sneaking off to meet in tunnels. Was there a . . . special one?"

Since there hadn't actually been *any* boy, much less a special one, I wasn't sure what to say. Finally I settled on, "I didn't have a boyfriend, if that's what you're asking."

"I was trying not to be that tacky about it, but yes, I was asking if you had . . . or if you *have* a boyfriend."

My heart was pounding fast now. This time I couldn't tell myself he was being friendly, or that this was "just Dex." Boys don't ask if you have a boyfriend unless they are interested in you.

And then something else occurred to me. I could tell him I did. Invent some long-distance guy, someone I e-mailed and Skyped with. And that would be that. Dex and I could be friends, nothing more. He might feel a little disappointed, and maybe he'd pull back a little.

Just the thought of that hurt. I hadn't known Dex very long, but I liked him. Genuinely. Hanging out with Romy was fun, but it wasn't the same as the time I spent with Dex.

I'd been quiet too long. "So that's a yes, then?" he asked, his voice every bit as light as mine had been moments ago. But I heard the hurt creeping around the edges.

Tell him yes. Tell him yes.

Turning around, I let the beam of my flashlight fall on the floor. "No. I don't have a boyfriend."

I thought I'd seen every one of Dex's smiles. The goofy one, the ironic one, the delighted one. But the grin that broke across his face was a whole new specimen: the sexy one.

"Oh, thank God," he breathed, and then he was crossing the cave and pulling me to him.

CHAPTER 26

Dex was taller than me, and as he pressed me against him, he actually hauled me up on my tiptoes. His arm was around my waist, his other hand plunged into my hair, and he was kissing me. I mean, really, really kissing me.

I was kissing him back. And I was *good* at it.

I didn't know if it was the spell, or if I was some kind of kissing prodigy. Everything I'd worried about—weird head movements, awkward lip placement, the Spit Dilemma—none of it was an issue. Dex and I kissed like we'd been doing it forever. That buzz I felt every time I touched him was still there, but now it was wrapped up in all these other feelings, feelings that seemed a lot more potent than any magic.

My fingers curled against his shoulders, the material of his jacket as soft as it had looked, and I shivered.

When we finally broke apart, his eyes were bluer than normal. He seemed dazed—and I wasn't feeling particularly clearheaded either. "Izzy," he murmured.

I pulled back. "It's a spell."

Dex blinked twice, shaking his head. "What?"

I was still trying to catch my breath. Trying to keep myself from jumping back into his arms. "This place. It's got some kind of love spell thing happening. That's the only reason we . . . we, uh . . ."

I was moving back toward him, my hands already itching to grab his lapels. One of his fingers curled around my belt loop, pulling me in, but before our lips could meet again, I slammed both of my palms against his chest. "You don't really want to kiss me," I blurted out.

"I . . . I'm sorry, what?"

Stepping back, I crossed my arms. "This cave. Someone did a love spell here. That's what all this—" I went to point to his hand, but it was empty now. Somewhere in the middle of . . . everything, Dex had dropped the heart charm. Clearing my throat, I rushed on. "Anyway, love spells are, like, crazy powerful. They can . . . seep into places. Make other people feel the effects of the magic. That's what's happening to us."

I was babbling and I knew it, but I just wanted to find something I could say that would erase the dawning horror on Dex's face.

"So . . . we kissed because of *magic*?"

"Right," I said, relieved. "So it doesn't mean anything."

His expression twisted, and now he didn't seem horrified. He seemed . . . *angry*.

"Is this something else you learned on the Internet?" he asked, his voice cold. "The effects of love spells on people who don't like each other?"

Confused, I shook my head. "I do like you."

Dex laughed, but it was a laugh I'd never heard him use before. It was sarcastic and harsh. "Of course you do. As a friend, right?" And then suddenly, all the anger seemed to drain out of him. He ran a hand over the top of his head, ruffling his hair. "Look, it's fine. We kissed because magic made us do it. Whatever. Let's just . . . let's just go."

He moved toward the tunnel and made what I thought was another harsh laugh. But it wasn't. It was a cough. Then a wheeze. And suddenly he was sliding to the floor, his shoulders and chest working, but no air coming in or going out.

I rushed over to him, thrusting my hands into the pockets of his jacket, but he shoved me off.

"I know things are weird with us, but now is *not the time*!" I shouted. In the dim glow of the flashlight I could see the skin around his lips turning blue. Dex made another wheeze, but this one sounded like it was trying to be a laugh. "Car," he mouthed.

I was bolting out of the cave the second the word was out of his mouth. Ducking to keep from whacking my head, I crawled faster than anyone has ever crawled before. By the time I got out to the car my hands were shaking. I yanked open the door and started pawing through the glove box. All that got me was a box of tissues and some hard peppermints.

Every bad word I knew was spilling from my lips as I thrust my hands between the seats. Finally, my fingers closed over metal, and I could've wept with relief when I pulled out Dex's inhaler.

When I got back to him, the wheezing had given way to a terrifying silence. Fumbling, I shoved the inhaler at him, sinking back on my heels when I heard him take several deep pulls on it.

It took much longer than it had that day on the football field, but after several agonizing seconds, Dex started breathing again. Color rushed back into his face, and he closed his eyes, shaking.

"Well, that was different," he whispered once he could finally talk. He opened one eye. "Never had an asthma attack from making out. You are one heck of a kisser, Izzy Brannick."

I would have hit him, but I was so glad he wasn't

dying that I just patted his shoulder instead. "I think it was the arguing rather than the kissing."

"Heh," he breathed. "Maybe." Both eyes opened. "I'm sorry, by the way. I shouldn't have gotten so pissed, but—"

"Forget about it," I said. "And . . . maybe it wasn't just the magic that made me kiss you. But, Dex. I can't . . . we can't . . ."

I didn't know what else to say. That seemed to sum it all up. I couldn't. *We* couldn't. My life was full of ridiculously dangerous stuff. And Dex, in his own way, was ridiculously brave. I thought about the clothes he wore, the unabashed affection he showed toward me, Romy, even his Nana. Every day of his life, Dex was uniquely himself, and he didn't care what people said about it. And I knew that if he really knew what my life was like, he'd want to be a part of it. That was the kind of guy he was—all in.

And being "all in" with me would get him killed.

"It's fine," Dex said, breathing more slowly. "As long as we can be friends, I'm . . . I'm good with that."

"Me, too," I said. And even though I knew that was true, I wondered why it made me so sad.

CHAPTER 27

"So . . . Everton likes Leslie?" Romy asked around a mouthful of popcorn.

"Yeah. Loves her, actually. But that was before the amnesia."

We were sitting in Romy's room on Saturday night, a big bowl of popcorn on the floor, two different kinds of sodas on her desk, and all three seasons of *Ivy Springs* sitting beside her TV.

I'd filled in her on what had happened at the cave. Well, the love spell part. Not the me and Dex kissing bit. Romy had told me about her and Anderson finding salt on the grave—and I tried to act very surprised about that—but in the end, both of us agreed that Friday night's field trips had been pretty successful, all things considered.

Then we'd put in *Ivy Springs* and let the trials of Leslie

and Everton distract us from our failure. Romy had already changed into her pajamas—naturally, they had cute little ghosts on them—and I was painting my toenails. Well, trying to. Since I'd never done it before, my feet looked like I'd accidentally stepped into a meat grinder. As I dabbed at the bright scarlet mess, Romy glanced up.

"Whoa," she said, eyes going wide. "What have you done?"

Sighing, I yanked a tissue out of the box on Romy's nightstand and began trying to wipe off the worst of it. "I think I used too much."

Romy laughed as she sat up. "Think? Iz, it looks like you poured half the bottle on your foot. Here, give me that." She snatched tissues away from me and rummaged in her nightstand drawer until she emerged with a bottle of nail polish remover. I reached for it, but she held her arm over her head. "Uh-uh. You cannot be trusted with dangerous chemicals, clearly. Give me your foot."

Hesitantly, I stretched out my leg, and Romy doused a few tissues with the polish remover. As she went to work scrubbing the worst of the mess off my right foot, she glanced at me over the top of her glasses. "You've never painted your toenails before, have you?"

I thought about lying, but seeing as how I'd somehow managed to get It's a Bit Chili in Here *between* my toes, I didn't think Romy would buy it.

"No. My mom is really strict about makeup."

Giving a low whistle, Romy shook her head. "Never played dodgeball, never been kissed, never used makeup . . ."

My face was nearly as scarlet as my toes. Well, my whole foot, actually.

When I didn't say anything, Romy raised her eyes. "Izzy?" she prompted.

I cleared my throat and tucked a strand of hair behind my ear. I hadn't planned on telling Romy about the kissing, but my stupid fair skin had given me away yet again. "I, um . . . me and Dex, we—"

Romy sat up so quickly she nearly turned over the bottle of polish remover. I caught it, but she didn't seem to notice since she was too busy clapping and squealing something that sounded like, "Ohmygodohmygodohmygodohmygod!"

Leaping off the bed, she paused the *Ivy Springs* DVD just as Everton was about to kiss Lila, Leslie's identical cousin. "I cannot believe we've been sitting here for an entire hour, painting nails and watching TV, when you could have been telling me every last detail about yours and Dexter O'Neil's mega-hot makeout session."

"It wasn't like that," I protested. "It was . . . Okay, it was exactly like that, but—"

Romy cut me off with another squeal, and I couldn't

236

help but laugh. "This is so very excellent," she said, flopping back down on the bed. "So when? Where? How?"

I drew back my now-polish-free foot, wrapping my arms around my knees. "Last night, at the cave, and, um, with our mouths?"

Romy rolled her eyes and hit me with one of the bright green throw pillows covering her bed. "I figured that last part. I just meant did he kiss you first, or beneath that shy exterior, are you secretly a seductive vixen?" She waggled her eyebrows, and now it was my turn to toss a pillow at her.

"He kissed me. Well, he asked me if I had a boyfriend, and I said no, and then we . . . kissed."

Telling it like that, it sounded so flat, so uneventful. But I didn't know how girls talked about this kind of thing. And besides, I kind of wanted to keep it private. It was almost like I was afraid if I shared all the details—how warm his lips had been, the softness of his jacket under my hands—it wouldn't feel as special anymore. And since it was probably the only time it was ever going to happen, I wanted it to stay special for a long time.

Something must have shown on my face, because Romy's giddy grin slipped into a puzzled frown. "Why did you make Sad Face?"

Before I could say anything, Romy rushed on. "Was it bad? I mean, I always thought Dex would be pretty good at kissing despite his general spazziness, but I could be wrong, and if I am, just tell me. I know he's my Boy Best Friend, but you're my *Girl* Best Friend, and that trumps him—"

I help up my hand like that could stop the rush of words. "No, it was not bad. And . . . I'm your best friend?" I'd never had a best friend unless you counted Finley. But even though she'd been my sister, and I'd loved her, it wasn't like we'd ever painted each other's toenails, and I shuddered to think of what she would've said about *Ivy Springs*.

Romy smiled, almost shyly. "Um, duh, of course you're my best friend. What do you think all this means"—she waved her hand, taking in the popcorn, the polish, the TV—"if not your initiation into Best Friendom?"

In my head, I could hear Mom's voice: *These people are not your friends, Izzy. They are a means to an end, and as soon as this job is over, you'll never see them again.*

But Romy was my friend. When she'd asked me to spend the night, I hadn't agreed so that I could pump her for more information about the hauntings. I'd said yes because I'd wanted to hang out with her. To paint nails and talk about boys and watch Everton and Leslie make idiots of themselves.

"Okay, see, there you go with Sad Face again," Romy said, and I sighed. "It's just . . . the kiss with Dex was good. And I like him. Lots. But I can't exactly do the boyfriend thing."

Now it was Romy's turn for Sad Face. "Why not?"

Because I'm a monster hunter and this whole thing was just a job and I have to tell my mom that Dex isn't really Prodigium soon and then she'll make us leave.

The words were right there, desperate to tumble out of my mouth in one big avalanche of overshare.

Instead I shrugged and said, "I need to concentrate on school. You know. For, um, SATs. And college. And . . . stuff like that."

I expected Romy to argue, but she just sighed and picked up the nail polish remover. "I get that," she said. "But it sucks. You guys seem like a weird fit at first glance, but I don't know. I think you'd be good together."

"Yeah," I replied.

And then I got off the bed and restarted *Ivy Springs* before Sad Face became Crying Face.

"Isolde. Isolde. ISOLDE."

Blinking, I sat up. Ugh, another Torin dream. Something I was definitely not in the mood for. "Go'way," I mumbled at him. "Don't wanna play dress-up."

But when I flopped over onto my stomach, I realized I wasn't in a ball gown. I also wasn't in a ballroom or on a boat. I was lying on the trundle bed in Romy's room, and Torin wasn't in my dreams, he was in her mirror.

Fully awake, I shot out of the bed and made my way as quietly as possible to Torin. My face nearly against the glass, I hissed, "What are you *doing*?"

"Dropping in," he said, raising his hands innocently. "Isn't that what blokes are supposed to do? Raid slumber parties?"

"No," I shot back, my voice barely audible. "At least I don't think so. But it doesn't matter. *You* should not be here."

Behind me, Romy made a snuffling noise in her sleep and turned over. I didn't think it was possible to be any quieter, but I tried anyway. "Go. Away."

"I miss you," he said suddenly. Our faces were very close to each other, and even though I knew it was impossible, I could've sworn I felt a puff of breath on my cheek. "You never talk to me anymore. And that?" He pointed to the stack of *Ivy Springs*, eyes narrowing. "Traitor."

"This is my job," I told him, ignoring the pang of guilt in my chest. What was wrong with me? I didn't have anything to feel guilty for. So I chose to watch the show with a real girl my own age instead of a four-hundred-year-old warlock trapped in a mirror. Surely, that wasn't anything to feel guilty about. Or at least I thought it wasn't. *Sassy Miss* hadn't exactly covered that.

"These people aren't a job to you anymore, Isolde," Torin said, voice low. "They're your friends. And while it causes me actual physical pain to admit this, your mum is right. In the end, getting close to humans can only hurt you."

I backed away from the glass, but he kept going. "I've watched generations of Brannick women get close to regular people. Fall in love, make friends. It ended in tragedy every single time, Isolde. I know you don't believe a large percentage of what I say, but believe that I have no desire to ever see you hurt. And these people will hurt you."

Romy rolled over again, and I looked back at her. "Romy is . . . she couldn't hurt me."

"Could she not?" In the glass, Torin walked over to Romy's desk and opened the top drawer, pulling out something thin and golden.

My heart sank, but I made myself cross the room and open that same drawer. There, hidden under a stack of purple Post-its, was a charm bracelet. There was a ballet slipper and a tiny golden unicorn and horseshoe and what I think was supposed to be a pot of gold. And in between the slipper and the unicorn was a space where, I had an awful feeling, a heart was supposed to go.

I put the bracelet back where I found it, silently slid the drawer closed, and walked back to the mirror. "It makes sense," Torin said as soon as I was in front of him.

"She finds a harmless little love spell somewhere, decides to try it out. And then she tries another spell, and another. And what do you know, she runs a ghost-hunting club, but there are no ghosts. So she works a little hedge magic, does a summoning or two. Just to make things interesting. And then it very quickly gets out of hand."

I wanted to deny it. To say there had to be some mistake. But Torin was right. It made total sense.

"What do I do?" I asked, but I wasn't sure if I was talking to Torin or myself.

"Tell your mum. Or tell that bloody Prodigium Council and let them deal with it. Let this girl know there are consequences for messing about with the unknown."

Both of those were technically good ideas, but they made my stomach twist in really awful ways. What if it turned out the only way to break this particular spell was to kill her? Mom would do that. If it was the only way, I had no doubt she could. And as for the Council . . . my cousin Sophie may have been in charge, but she wasn't there right now. Who knew what those people would do to Romy?

"I can't," I said, and Torin watched me with an unreadable expression.

Finally he said, "This is being a Brannick, Izzy. No one said it would be easy."

And with that, he was gone.

CHAPTER 28

First thing Sunday morning I faked an upset stomach and left Romy's. She seemed a little down, but I let her keep the last season of *Ivy Springs*, which cheered her up. Instead of home, I headed for the library. Unfortunately, Ideal's library wasn't exactly the best resource, and I quickly saw why Mom had needed to drive three towns over to get her books. Looking for anything on "hedge magic" only got me a bunch of volumes on how to grow hedges. Thinking of Dex's horrible lawn, I wondered if I should check one out for Nana. Then I remembered that everything between me and Dex was kind of awful right now. Besides, I had the case to focus on.

That night, Mom and I went back to that Chinese place, and I told her I was ready to leave. She raised her eyebrows. "Case closed?"

"Almost," I said. I still hadn't figured out how to stop Romy. Part of me wondered if I could just talk to her like . . . like a friend. Or maybe sneak a fake article into *American Teen* that said something like, "Why Hedge Magic and Raising Ghosts Is So Last Year!"

By Monday, I still hadn't found anything. Dex had saved me a seat on the bus like usual, but he was very careful not to sit too close to me. I think both of us were relieved when Romy turned around and started telling Dex about her and Anderson's night.

"And there was salt, like, everywhere," she said, pushing her glasses up. "I mean, that was all we saw, but that has to mean something, right?"

Dex made a sort of choked laugh that he quickly turned into a cough. Romy's brow furrowed. "You okay?"

"Yeah, just . . . Anyway, Izzy, why don't you fill Romy in on our night?"

"She already did," Romy said, barely suppressing a smile. She winked at me, and I wanted to be able to wink back so badly. Instead, I reached into my pocket. "I left out a part. We also found this." Before leaving the cave Friday night, I'd searched the floor for that heart charm. I pulled it out of my pocket now.

Romy plucked the charm from my hand, a weird expression on her face. As she studied it, I studied *her*. "Have you seen it before?"

Startled, she raised her head. "I have a charm kind of like this, but it doesn't look all blackened and stuff." She handed it back to me. "Maybe it belonged to Mary."

I don't know what I'd expected. Not for her to be like, "Oh, right, this is mine! I did some kind of freaky spell at that cave, and whoops! Now we're plagued by ghosts." But I'd thought she'd show a little more reaction than that. If anything, she just seemed kind of confused.

We had a test in English and a freaking relay race in P.E., so I didn't get a chance to talk to her any more that morning. Then she didn't show up at lunch, so I made up my mind to talk to her during history, only to find out class wasn't meeting because there was a pep rally for the basketball team. There had been, like, eight in the first season of *Ivy Springs*, but I'd never actually been to one. And I have to admit, my curiosity to see what an actual pep rally looked like almost outweighed my need to know what was up with Romy.

The gym was already full by the time we got there, but Romy and Anderson had saved a couple of places at the very top of the bleachers, just like the night of the basketball game. Dodging other kids, Dex and I carefully made our way up there. At one point, I nearly stumbled and he reached out, catching my hand. It was the first time we'd touched since the cave, and the feel of his hand on mine made me remember his lips on mine, his hands on my back. But the instant I had righted myself, Dex dropped my hand.

It was for the best. Really. Dex and I couldn't be together, not like that. And I wouldn't be at the school for much longer. The less I had to miss, the better.

Once we reached the top of the bleachers, I sat by Romy, and Dex went over beside Anderson. Even with two people between us, I was so aware of him my skin felt charged.

Trying to take my mind off of that, I nodded down at the gym floor. "So what exactly is going to happen?" I asked Romy.

She turned to me, surprised. "You've seriously never been to a pep rally?"

"They, uh, didn't do them at my old school. We didn't have sports." I was too distracted to sound sincere, but Romy didn't seem to notice.

"Okay, well, basically, it's a stupid and pointless ritual wherein we all cheer for our stupid, pointless basketball team. We'll shout some stuff, the cheerleaders will do a dance, and then the mascot will come out and we'll shout some more."

"That sounds . . . dumb."

Romy nodded. "It is. Intensely. But it's better than history, I guess."

At that, the basketball team, all wearing their

warm-up suits, jogged out into the gym and everyone started hooting and clapping like these weren't the same guys we saw every single day. About half the kids in the bleachers even leapt to their feet, but since Romy, Anderson, and Dex all stayed seated, so did I.

The band started up, and I saw Adam on the very edge, playing his drum. I'd kept a close eye on him since the locker thing, but so far there had been no sign of Mary. I wasn't even sure what she was planning for him. Snyder had gotten the frog with the bashed-in head, signaling that he was about to get his head bashed in. Beth had gotten the mangled Barbie a few days before she was nearly hit by a car. Adam had gotten an explosion. A month ago, I would have said a ghost making someone blow up was pretty much impossible, but if Mary could wield a killer microscope and manipulate a car, what was to stop her from sending Adam sky high? Still, I wondered how she was going to manage that, exactly.

Dex leaned closer to Anderson. I heard him murmur something, and all thoughts of Adam were forgotten.

Maybe I could try to talk to Dex on the bus. Tell him . . . I don't know, I'd lied about not having a boyfriend. And then I'd felt guilty about the kiss, and that's why I'd spazzed out. He was probably too smart to buy that, but it was worth a try. God, why were boys so complicated? I suddenly wished I had a ghost to fight right that second. Or a vampire. A werewolf. Heck, I'd even take a gollum, no matter how messy killing one was. Anything to make me feel like me again.

I sat there brooding through the rest of the pep rally. It worked pretty much exactly like Romy had said, and I had nearly tuned it out by the time the giant hedgehog rushed onto the court.

On the other side of Romy and Anderson, Dex snorted, and in that moment I wanted nothing more than to be sitting beside him, hearing whatever snarky comments he undoubtedly made about the mascot.

I hadn't realized I was staring at him until he turned his head and looked at me. Romy and Anderson were talking, their heads close together, but for a second it was like there wasn't anyone but me and Dex. A little smile drifted across his face, and just when I was thinking about returning it, there was a shout from the gym floor.

The hedgehog was wheeling out a big "cannon." As one of the cheerleaders handed him a sparkler, I leaned over and asked Romy, "What's the deal with that?"

She rolled her eyes. "Ugh, this is the *big finale* every time. He pretends to light the fuse, and then it shoots out glitter and confetti while we all ooh and ahh and pretend he hasn't done it a million times. On the upside, it means this stupid pep rally is almost over."

"So it's not a real cannon?" I asked.

Romy shook her head. "Nope. Just an air cannon."

"But . . ." I leaned forward. "It *looks* like a real one. Like that one that's outside the front of the school."

The hedgehog took the sparkler as the student body stomped their feet, chanting, "M! E! H! S!" He lit the fuse, and it kindled, smoking.

I sat up straighter. "Did he just really light that?"

Squinting, Romy peered down. "Huh. Yeah. Maybe this is a new part of the routine."

But the cheerleader who'd handed the mascot the sparkler was staring at the fuse in confusion. Then she started backing up, saying something over her shoulder to one of the other cheerleaders. And the hedgehog, suddenly looking a lot more malevolent than I'd ever thought a hedgehog could, pushed on the barrel of the cannon until it was pointing straight at the band. Or, more specifically, straight at Adam. I saw him drop his drumsticks, face wrinkling in confusion. A group of kids cheered, obviously expecting glitter and confetti, like Romy had said.

Shooting to my feet, I tried to make my way down the bleachers, but I was too high up and there were too many people. Distantly, I heard Dex call my name, but I was too busy trying to get to the floor.

One of the cheerleaders was shouting and pointing at the cannon, and I heard a chorus of shrieks go up from the gym floor. I wasn't going to make it.

But then, a basketball player darted from the first row of the bleachers, throwing all his weight onto the cannon. The sound its wheels made on the hardwood was awful, but the deafening boom that followed was much, much worse.

Thanks to the basketball player, the explosion pounded into the far wall of the gym instead of Adam—and all the kids within fifty feet of him. But it didn't matter. Everything descended into complete pandemonium as kids screamed at and shoved each other, trying to get off the bleachers and out of the gym. I hung on to the railing, inching down the side of the bleachers. Down on the floor, one of the basketball players was holding the hedgehog's arms behind its back as another boy reached up and tugged the mascot's head off.

The suit was empty.

As the boy holding the head staggered back, the suit slid through the other player's arms, pooling onto the floor.

I only *thought* there had been panic before. The screaming got louder, people started shoving harder, and the entire building seemed to quake.

Fear—thick, choking waves of it—rushed through the gym. More than fear, really. Terror. Horror. Dread. All of it pulsing in the air, and somewhere, I knew, Mary Evans was getting stronger.

Much stronger.

CHAPTER 29

Since the school had been evacuated, we held the emergency meeting of PMS at Romy's house. Romy's mom had gone overboard with the snack options, laying out three different kinds of chips on the counter, as well as two kinds of soft drinks.

Once we'd gotten our food we followed Romy up to her room.

Romy immediately clambered onto her bed, sitting cross-legged in the middle. Anderson sat next to her, while I took the desk chair and Dex folded his long body onto a bright green beanbag chair.

"Okay," Romy said, dusting crumbs off her hands, "I think we can all agree there's some seriously crazy stuff going on at Mary Evans High."

"I don't know, Rome," Dex said, crossing his ankles.

"Hedgehog violence is a lot more common than you'd think."

"What I still don't get," Anderson said, grabbing a handful of chips, "is why she went from floating some chalk to this whole reign of terror thing."

"There never was a haunting before," I said, finally getting it. "Floating chalk, locker doors opening, all of that was BS, just stories people told." I was too freaked out and thinking too fast to even pretend I didn't know much about the paranormal. "This is the only haunting Mary Evans High has ever had, and it's because someone used magic and freaking summoned a ghost."

All three of them stared at me, but I didn't care anymore. This had gone too far, and after what had happened in the gym today, Mary would be stronger than ever. We didn't have any more time.

I took a deep breath. It had come to this. "And I think I know who."

I walked over to Romy's desk and pulled out her bracelet, dangling it on one finger as my other hand fished in my pocket for the charm I'd found in the cave. "This belongs to you, doesn't it?" I asked her.

Very carefully, Romy put her can of soda down. "Yeah. What are you saying?"

I could feel Anderson's and Dex's eyes on me as I said, "You run a ghost-hunting club, but you didn't have any ghosts to hunt. So maybe you stumbled across a spell somewhere. Hedge magic," I said. "You just thought you'd call up a couple of local spirits. Nothing too dangerous, nothing that could hurt anyone. But hedge magic can be tricky, and something went wrong. And people *are* getting hurt, Romy."

Her face was a mask as she took all of that in. Finally, she got off the bed and snatched the bracelet out of my hand. "That is my bracelet, and yes, that *is* my charm. But I lost it weeks ago. I certainly wasn't hanging out in a cave, conjuring up 'hedge magic.' And what does that even *mean*?"

"It's something—"

"Don't say you read it on the Internet."

"You *do* say that a lot," Dex said, and for once he didn't sound like he was joking. In fact, I could swear that was actual suspicion on his face as he watched me. "First the salt thing, now witches summoning ghosts . . .'"

Romy was looking at me weird, too. "What salt thing?"

Glaring at Dex, I said, "It was nothing. And besides, it didn't work."

"All this stuff did start happening when you showed up," Anderson said, his voice very quiet. I threw up my hands.

"What the heck? You said you'd been investigating

253

the Mary Evans thing since Mr. Snyder. And that was months ago."

"There weren't any hedgehogs trying to blow up the gym months ago," Anderson offered.

"It has nothing to do with me," I insisted, but even as I said it, a shiver ran down my spine. That was true. They'd had one incident before I came here. Now all hell had broken loose. Had I somehow unleashed all of this?

"You seem to know an awful lot about ghosts for someone who claims to not care about the paranormal," Romy spit out.

Anderson was nodding slowly, and even Dex seemed troubled. "The thing with the salt," he repeated. "The day after that, Beth ended up nearly becoming roadkill."

"I was trying to trap Mary's ghost," I fired back. "Not help her kill Beth."

It was the wrong thing to say. Anderson's face went hard. "You saw her at the graveyard the night before Beth nearly got mowed down?" he asked Dex.

Dex nodded. "She did say she was trying to keep the ghost in the grave."

"Which clearly didn't work."

"If I were trying to get Beth killed, why would I have saved her life?"

"Like you said, you didn't want anyone to get hurt," Romy said. "You felt guilty."

"No, I didn't!" I said. Or rather, yelled. Romy actually flinched. Trying to soften my tone, I added, "I didn't feel guilty because I have nothing to feel guilty about. I didn't call forth any ghosts. You did."

"No," Romy said through clenched teeth, "I. Didn't."

"Okay, fine," I said, so frustrated I wanted to shake her. "You didn't. Some other person came in here and stole your bracelet and started doing spells all over the place. The point is, we need to stop it. This ghost is dangerous, Romy. And you can't stop her with a blinking box and a tinfoil hat."

Romy swung an accusatory glare at Dex. "Stop talking about the hat."

"*That's* what you're choosing to be upset about?"

"If our blinking boxes and tinfoil hats are so stupid to you, Izzy, maybe you shouldn't be in PMS anymore," Anderson said.

I was surprised at how much that stung. And even more surprised that Dex stayed quiet. When I looked over at him in the beanbag chair, he was staring at the carpet, chewing his thumbnail.

"Fine," I said, wishing my voice hadn't wavered. "Go ahead. Deal with the crazy, murderous ghost on your own. I was just trying to help."

"We don't need your help," Romy said, and to my horror, my eyes started watering. Before the group could see that, I grabbed my backpack and, with as much dignity as I could muster, walked out of Romy's room, closing the door behind me.

The walk to my house didn't take long, but with every step, I got angrier and angrier. This is what happened when you get involved with regular kids. Stupid kids, who summoned a ghost and probably were going to get killed by it. And that was fine. That's what happened when people messed with stuff that was way over their heads. So sue me for trying to step in and use, oh, I don't know, *a thousand years of bloodline and experience and training* to keep them safe. Let them wear their tinfoil hats. And let Dex—

The tears nearly spilled over then, but I stopped just outside my front door and took a deep breath. No. I wasn't going to cry over him.

Them. Whatever.

Mom's car was parked in the driveway, so I called out for her when I went inside.

"In here," she answered from the kitchen.

I walked down the hall, and was surprised to find Maya standing next to the sink with Mom.

"What are you—" I started to say, but before I could get out any more, Mom turned to me. She wasn't smiling, but her eyes were practically shining. "It's Finn," she said. "We got a lead on Finn."

CHAPTER 30

"What?" was all I could say.

Moving quickly, Mom grabbed her jacket from a kitchen chair. "A girl just a few counties over disappeared last week. Same as Finley. Got involved with a coven of dark witches and vanished."

"Oh," I said, trying to keep the disappointment out of my voice. The news was great, better than anything we'd gotten so far. But it didn't seem like much. For some reason, when Mom said she had a lead, I thought it would mean . . . more. That we could have Finley back tonight.

I suddenly wanted that more than anything in the world. Finn and I had fought, and maybe we'd never painted our nails together, but she hadn't lied to me. She hadn't summoned ghosts and then called *me* a freak.

"Anyway, Maya is going to stay here with you until I

get back. Should be later tonight, maybe early tomorrow morning."

"I don't need a babysitter," I said, but Mom waved that off.

"Not now, Izzy. With everything that's been going on, I'd rather you didn't stay here alone."

"Besides," Maya said, moving to the stove, where she was boiling something that smelled like rosemary and death, "we'll have a big time. I can braid your hair, teach you a few incantations . . ."

I gave the least enthusiastic "Yay" of all time.

"As soon as I get back, we'll deal with your hedge witch friend, and then we can get home," Mom said, startling me.

I whirled around to face Mom. "You know? How?"

Flipping her hair over the collar of her coat, Mom glanced out toward the hall. "Torin is not always completely useless."

No, but he *was* completely slimy and untrustworthy. "He shouldn't have told you," I insisted. "This is my case, and I'm handling it."

"It was your case when it was a run-of-the-mill haunting. Or figuring out what kind of Prodigium that boy was. Which you never did, apparently."

"I was working on it," I told her, but Mom frowned.

"It's time to put an end to this entire case, Iz, and

you're too involved. As soon as I get back, we're finishing it. Besides, it's getting dangerous."

"It hasn't been *that* dangerous," I said, conveniently ignoring the whole pyromaniac hedgehog thing.

But Mom shook her head. "You're done. If we can't put a stop to this haunting now, it's only going to get worse. The more afraid people get, the stronger that ghost will become, and the stronger she becomes, the more people she can hurt. If we're not careful, this will become a cycle that pretty much can't be stopped."

"How will you stop Mary?" I asked Mom, and her eyes slide from mine.

"Stay here with Maya, and when I get back, we'll fix this."

"*You'll* fix this, you mean," I muttered.

Normally, that would've gotten me a sharp "Isolde!" and a remark about talking back. But to my surprise, this time, Mom just crossed the kitchen and laid her palm against my cheek. "You've done great here. You've proven yourself, and I am proud of you. But it's time to walk away now."

The last time Mom had touched my face I'd been ten years old and she'd thought I had a fever. That must've been why I just nodded and said, "Okay."

Mom dropped her hand with a little smile. "Good."

Turning to Maya, she lifted a canvas bag off the table. "I'll call from the road."

"Bring her home, Ash," Maya said, stirring her concoction.

"I'm going to try," Mom replied, and with one last look at me, she was gone.

As soon as the front door closed, Maya opened a cabinet and began pulling out a couple of bowls. "You want some?" she asked, gesturing to the stove.

"Um . . . no. I've got something to do."

Before she could offer me anything else—eye of newt tea, bird's feet stew—I took off to the guest room.

Once the door was shut behind me I marched over to Torin's mirror, smacking the frame as hard as I could. He stumbled, falling against the bed. "What in the world are you doing?"

"Don't." I pointed at him. "I wanted to figure out what to do about Romy on my own. I trusted you."

"And I was only trying to help," he insisted. "You could've been hurt, and for what? A trio of ungrateful children? They turned on you, didn't they." It wasn't a question.

His words stung, but I tried not to let it show. "They didn't turn on me. They had every reason to suspect I was a freak because hey, news flash, I *am* a freak. It doesn't make them ungrateful. It makes them . . . smart."

Torin frowned. "Isolde—"

I reached out and covered his mirror, suddenly tired and sadder than I'd thought possible.

After trudging up the stairs I spent the rest of the afternoon putting my few belongings back in the duffel bag, and watching the last few episodes of *Ivy Springs*, season three. But somehow, even Everton and Leslie finally getting together (and riding off in a hot air balloon, which may have been even weirder than the episode where Leslie dreamed she and Everton were on the *Titanic*) still couldn't cheer me up. Once it was dark, I decided to go down to the kitchen and talk to Maya. Hopefully, she was done cooking.

She was humming when I walked in and puttering with the sad little basil plant Mom had bought at Walmart. It had been sitting, pathetic and abandoned, on our windowsill for a while.

"No bird's feet, I'm guessing?" Maya asked as I walked in.

"Fresh out," I told her. Now that the kitchen no longer smelled like Evil Magic, I thought I might try to cook some dinner. Maybe carbs would cheer me up where *Ivy Springs* had failed. As I pulled out a box of macaroni and cheese, Maya gave a cheerful smile.

"No matter," she said, heading for the fruit bowl in the middle of the table. I'd just done the grocery shopping a few days ago, so there were several apples and a couple of bananas in there. My pasta forgotten, I watched as Maya picked up two apples and one banana and laid them on either side of the basil plant. Muttering something under her breath, she held on to the little pot of basil, and the leaves began to turn green and bright. But as they did, the apples and banana shriveled, going brown.

Once the basil was as perky as it could possibly be, Maya reached up and took off one of the several silver hoops in her ears. "That's . . . bizarre," I said at last.

"Hedge magic!" she trilled with a little shrug.

I scowled. Real magic, hedge magic, all of it apparently led to the same place: with everything crappy and awful. But it wasn't just that. Something was bothering me. It made sense that Romy was the one summoning ghosts, whether she'd meant to or not, but there was still this little niggling doubt in the back of my mind. Romy was a terrible liar, but she'd looked genuinely confused and hurt in her bedroom today. And there hadn't been any guilt in her face when I'd shown her the heart charm, just puzzlement.

"Maya," I said as she continued to cluck over the plant, "let's say you have a hedge witch summoning ghosts, and the one she's summoned is all big and scary and dangerous."

Maya turned back to me, her eyes sad. "Honey, most of the time, you can just get a witch to send the ghost back herself."

Breathing a sigh of relief, I sat the box of pasta on the counter. "That's what I'd been thinking—"

"But," Maya interrupted. "This is not a normal case. The ghost is too powerful. By this point, the only way to stop that ghost is to sever the connection with the witch who did the summoning. Hedge witch, 'real' witch, it doesn't matter. Stop the witch, you stop the ghost."

I tore open the box of macaroni even though I was far from hungry anymore. "And by stop, you mean . . ."

"Kill, yes." She touched one of the charms around her neck. "It's unfortunate, but that's the way of it."

My feet were bare, and when I looked down I saw my bright red toenails. A lump rose in my throat. "She made a mistake. She did a dumb thing, but she shouldn't have to pay for it with her life. There has to be some other way."

When I glanced up, Maya was wringing her hands. "What?"

"It's just . . ." She broke off, huffing out a breath. "Oh, your mama would kill me if she knew I was even whispering about this, but . . . there's maybe one way. To sever the connection without severing your friend's jugular."

I pushed the box of macaroni away. "Yeah, I'm going to need to hear about that."

"But it's dangerous and potentially unstable, and is really one of those tricks best left to those Pro-whatchamacallit witches."

Leaning forward, I pressed my hands on the counter. "Maya, whatever it is, I'll try it."

She filled me in on what exactly the ritual would require—and do—and while by the end of it, my heart was pounding and my eyes were huge, I agreed that it sounded a lot better than letting my mom run Romy through with a dagger.

"Okay," I said, pointing at Maya. "You go get the supplies you need, I'll call Romy and get her over here."

But when I dialed Romy's cell there was no answer. She was probably avoiding me, and I couldn't blame her. Luckily, I had her house number too, and I dialed that.

Romy's mom answered, and when I said who I was, she sounded surprised. "Oh! Izzy. I thought for sure you'd be out with the rest of them."

My heart lodged somewhere in my throat. "The rest of who?"

"The club. Romy said you'd called a special meeting tonight."

"Oh, right," I said, even as my grip threatened to shatter the phone. "I totally spaced. Could you remind me where it is?"

There was a pause, and then Romy's mom sighed and said, "God, Izzy, you are going to think I am the worst mother, but I honestly don't remember." She gave a little laugh. "Such is life with triplets, I guess."

I did my best to laugh back, but I couldn't get off the phone fast enough. Hanging up with her, I hesitated only the briefest second before dialing another number.

It picked up on the first ring. "Izzy?"

"Dex," I said, but before I could get anything else out, he rushed in.

"Izzy, I'm so sorry about what happened this afternoon. You know I—"

"DEX!" I said again, and mercifully, he stopped babbling. "Are you with Romy and Anderson?"

I could hear him sigh. "No. After you left, I may have quit the club. Very dramatically, I should add, complete with—"

I liked Dex. A lot. Heck, maybe I even more than liked him. But in a crisis, he was not exactly user-friendly. "Do you know where they were going tonight?"

"Yeah," he answered immediately, and I nearly sagged with relief. "They were going to the cave. You know, the one where we—"

"Right, right," I hurried on. "Okay, I think I've worked out a way we can stop Mary Evans without hurting Romy."

"I was unaware Romy getting hurt was ever on the table."

"It's not," I said, looking over my shoulder to where Maya was throwing every canister of salt we had into a duffel bag. *At least I hope it's not.*

"Do you want me to meet you there?"

There was no time to think, but I still hesitated, just for a little bit. I did want him to come with me. Because no matter how things went tonight, once everything was over, I'd leave Ideal. This was probably my last chance to see him.

"No." It came out like kind of a croak, and I cleared my throat. "No, there's no need for you to come. I just need to make things right with Romy."

"Okay," he said, his voice lower than usual. "Izzy—"

I hung up. Whatever he was going to say next would probably just make all of this harder than it was. Besides, Maya was ready and I needed to go.

"Thanks," I said, taking the bag and holding out my free hand. "If you'll just give me your keys—"

But Maya blocked the front door, hands on her wide hips. "No way," she said. "I promised your Mom I'd watch you, and letting you run off to fight a hedge witch and a homicidal ghost is probably one of those things she'd frown on. Besides, you'll need my help with the ritual."

Reminding myself that decking old ladies is wrong, I took a deep breath. "Maya, I appreciate that, but my friends are in danger, and I have to help them. On my own."

But instead of being impressed with what I thought was a pretty stoic delivery, Maya laughed. "You Brannicks are always saying that." She dropped her voice an octave or so. "'I have to do this alone. This is my sole duty. I cannot accept help.'" Shaking her head, she said, "But you don't do it alone. You *never* have. There's always people like me, or that weirdo you keep in a mirror, or these kids at your school."

Leaning forward, she took me by the shoulders. "You aren't alone, Izzy. You or your mom or, when we find her, Finley. And whether you like it or not, you need help. And you're getting it. So get your skinny little butt in my car, and let's go kick some ghost ass."

CHAPTER 31

Anderson's car was parked outside of the cave when we pulled up. Leaning over the steering wheel, Maya whistled low. "Well, if this isn't the perfect setting for a ghost face-off, I don't know what is."

I looked into the mouth of the cave, but everything was dark. Still, they were in there, I was sure of it.

Getting out of the car, I walked to the trunk. Maya and I were just hefting out our bag of supplies when a splash of headlights lit up the gloom. "Who on earth—" Maya started, but I recognized the burgundy town car immediately.

Even though I should have been horrified, I couldn't stop the giddy leap of my heart or the sudden smile that wanted to break out over my face. The car stopped, and Dex loped out of the passenger side.

"I told you not to come," I said, walking over to him.

He threw up his hands. "And yet. Now, what are we doing here?"

He squinted past me at Maya, who was already toting the bag into the cave.

"Dex," I said, pushing my hands into my back pockets so I wouldn't do something stupid like hug him. "This could get— Wait, you didn't drive."

Running a hand up and down the back of his neck, Dex sighed. "Yes, my Nana had to drive me. You see, apparently, nearly being blown up at school was somehow my fault, so now I'm grounded. But when I explained that my Fair Isolde had need of me . . ."

I looked up into his blue eyes, taking in tonight's scarf, which was a riot of turquoise and purple. His curly black hair was sticking up, and oh man, he was right. I did need him. Kind of a lot.

Which was just so, so unfortunate.

"Dexter!" Nana called, rolling down her window.

"Ah, yes." He jogged back to the car, resting his hand on her windowsill and ducking his head inside. "Nana, Izzy needs me to go into this cave to get our friends. I'm going to help her with that, while you wait right here."

Nana smiled at me. "Hello, Izzy. Dexter, you know I always appreciate your being helpful, but this seems . . ."

She looked past us toward the cave, and Dex craned

his head over his shoulder, following her gaze. "I know it looks vaguely unsanitary and potentially scandalous, Nana, but I promise that Izzy and I are only pursuing noble . . . pursuits. We've even got a chaperone! Izzy, who was that woman who went into the cave?"

I blanked, not sure how to describe Maya. I settled on, "My . . . also my Nana."

"See?" Dex said brightly, ducking his head in to kiss his Nana's cheek. "Izzy's Nana! We are totally safe and appropriate."

I wasn't sure Nana was convinced, but she pursed her lips and said, "No longer than ten minutes, Dexter."

He gave her a jaunty salute, and we turned and walked into the mouth of the cave.

Maya was in the first chamber, spreading salt. It was to Dex's credit that he just took her in with a "Huh," and followed me deeper into the cave.

"Okay, so—" I started, but then his hand grasped my shoulders, turning me so that my back was against the cavern wall.

"I like you."

Bewildered, I blinked at him. "What?"

"I. Like. You," Dex repeated, and for once there was no glimmer in his eyes, no smile lurking on his lips. "I have since that morning on the track, and I should've made that clearer by now."

Somewhere in this cave, Romy and Anderson were very possibly in danger. "Dex, seriously, now is not the—"

"No," he said, giving me a little shake. "There is never going to be the right time, Izzy. I've figured that out by now. Every time I try to tell you this, you brush it off or don't let me finish, or someone tries to blow up the gym. So I'm telling you now. I like you. And it has nothing to do with spells or near-death excitement or any of the other BS excuses you like to come up with."

"Dex," I said again, helplessly.

"And you like me, too," he went on, and there, at last, was the smile. "That's not just me being arrogant, by the way. Although I understand that that's sometimes a problem. But"—he hurried on when I opened my mouth to reply—"I can work on that. If you want. Even though I think you secretly like that, too."

Maybe it was knowing that we were about to walk into something really scary. Maybe I was afraid that, even if I didn't get killed tonight, Dex might. Or maybe I just really wanted to kiss him. In any case, I fisted my hands in the front of his shirt and jerked him to me. Our lips met, and if this kiss wasn't as . . . thorough as the first one, it felt bigger somehow. More important.

"You're right," I panted, once I'd wrenched my mouth from his. "I like you. A lot. And I just wanted you to know that, too. But—"

Dex just kissed me again, a quick peck on the lips, really. "No," he whispered. "No buts. Now. Let's go get Romy and Anderson."

Almost as though his words had summoned it, there was a sudden flare of blue light from farther back in the cave system. "Crap," I muttered, tugging Dex's hand.

We followed a twisting, narrow path that finally opened up onto a bigger chamber. Keeping Dex behind me, I walked in, not sure what I was going to see.

But it was just Anderson, his back to us. Dex blew out a relieved breath. "Oh, there you are, man. We were—"

But then Anderson began backing up slowly, his hands held out at his sides. As he turned, we could see Romy standing in front of him. Blue light pulsed all around her, and Mary Evans suddenly appeared, standing just in front of Romy, almost like she was superimposed over her. She wore a long white dress, and her blond hair was plastered to her face.

Then Mary vanished, and Romy was there again, holding a long silver knife to Anderson's chest.

Dex hissed a four-letter word under his breath, and I held my arm out, keeping him behind me.

Romy glanced over at me, her face briefly becoming Mary's again. The effect was unsettling and awful. "I wanted you," she said, two voices coming out of Romy's mouth. "You felt strong and . . . different. I thought if I could get inside of you, I could burn the world."

I stepped back slightly, pushing Dex. "I'm actually not much of a fan of world burning, so . . ."

Romy laughed, and it echoed eerily in the cavern. "It doesn't matter. I can make this one pay." She jabbed at Anderson with the knife, and he gave a startled sound of pain.

"Anderson didn't do anything to you," I said, but she laughed again, shaking her head, her features flipping between Romy's and Mary's so quickly they blurred.

"No, but the men who did are dead."

"No one hurt you," Anderson said, his voice wavering. "Y-you died of exposure."

Grinning, Mary/Romy flicked the knife. One of the buttons on Anderson's shirt went flying off into the darkness.

"That's what they say, isn't it? That I froze, all alone, waiting for my child's father. A tragic fate, but not a cruel one. Freezing to death is supposed to be peaceful. Like slipping into a warm bath and then a long sleep." She stepped closer, and I saw the very tip of the knife pierce Anderson's chest. "But burning to death? That is very. Far. From. PEACEFUL."

She screamed the last word, and all of us cringed as it bounced off the rock walls. "That's what they did, you know," Mary said. She was completely Mary now, even though it was Romy's face and Romy's body. Romy's eyes had never radiated that much hate. "My father and his friends. When they found me playing at spells. Nothing dangerous, nothing harmful. Just a love charm to make the man I wanted mine."

Smiling, Mary kept advancing on Anderson even as he backed up. A thin trickle of blood ran down his shirt. "And do you know what these good, righteous men of Ideal, Mississippi, did? They dragged me to this cave, saying 'thou shalt not suffer a witch to live,' and they set me on fire."

"I'm so sorry," I said, and I was. I thought of that sweet, shy, smiling girl in the picture. She hadn't deserved to die like that. No one did. But that didn't mean I could let her hurt innocent people.

"And now," Mary continued, "I will make everyone suffer."

She lunged forward, but I was ready. Grabbing Anderson's arm, I spun him away from Mary, shoving him toward Dex and the passageway. Mary's blade sunk into my arm, the pain somehow icy cold and burning at the same time, but I gritted my teeth and struck out with my other hand. The blow sent her reeling backward. "That's the thing with possessing people," I said, pushing the boys out of the cavern. "People have *bodies*, which

274

makes them a lot easier to beat up than a ghost."

Mary screamed in rage, but I kept pushing Dex and Anderson, praying I'd given Maya the time she needed to set everything up.

We came tearing into the main cavern, our feet skidding on the salt covering the floor. Maya stood at the ready, and when Mary ran in, Maya shouted a word.

The effect was instant and painful. The whole cavern seemed to ring like a bell, and Mary shrieked, falling to her knees.

Once again, she started to flicker, part Mary, part Romy. Maya watched her, eyes wide.

"Where's the witch?"

"That's her," I said, breathing hard and pointing at Romy where she knelt on the ground. "The ghost is in her, it . . . it possessed her."

Maya was holding some kind of herbs in one hand and an ancient-looking book in the other. She let both drop to the ground. "Oh, hon," she said, so sad. "Then there's nothing I can do. The witch and the ghost, they have to be separate for this ritual to work."

Romy was writhing on the floor as though the salt was burning her. There was nothing of the girl I knew in her face, but I couldn't bear the thought of having to kill her. Not when she'd painted my toenails and made me laugh and been the first person I'd ever called friend.

Maya came to my side, holding out the small silver dagger she'd brought, *Just in case.*

Automatically, I tried to shove the dagger back toward her, but Maya gently pressed the hilt into my palm. "Sweetheart, she's in pain. A lot of it. If this doesn't work, you need to set her free."

Bile rose in my throat.

"Do you want me to do it?" Maya asked, and next to me, both Dex and Anderson stared.

"Do what?" Anderson asked just as Dex said, "I know you're not suggesting what—"

But I ignored them both. This was my fault. If I'd done something the instant I'd found out Romy had summoned Mary, maybe there would have been enough time. Maybe we could've fixed it before Mary got so strong. And if this didn't stop now, every person in Ideal would be in danger. Mary's rage would get stronger and stronger, her desire to hurt even more intense. This had to end.

And I had to be the one to end it.

My hand closed around the hilt of the dagger, but before I could take it from Maya, a voice rang out in the cave. "Dexter?"

The four of us turned slowly to see Dexter's Nana. She was wearing a sweatshirt embroidered with kittens, and the firelight turned her glasses into glowing orbs.

"Nana, I can explain," Dex said, as his gaze swung from me and the dagger back to Romy, crumpled on the floor, and back again.

"Oh, dear," Nana said, stepping forward. "I believe this may be all my fault."

CHAPTER 32

"Nana, how on earth could this be your fault?"

She nodded at Romy. "There's . . . there's a ghost in that young girl, isn't there?"

Dumbly, all four of us nodded.

Nana sniffed. "Yes, that's what I thought. Mary Evans. You know, she was the local legend when I was a girl growing up here. There were rumors she was a witch and . . ." She broke off with a chuckle. "Well, maybe I sympathized with her. I had always done the odd little charm myself."

She stopped suddenly, moving closer to Dex, who was watching her with a mixture of horror and confusion. "I didn't mean to do it." Her hand, as it cupped his cheek, was trembling. "But you were lying there on the floor, and you couldn't breathe."

Dex reared back slightly. "What?"

Nana shook her head, tears sliding down her face. "Your chest, it—it kept moving, but no air was getting in, and your eyes . . ." She gave a shuddering sigh. "Those beautiful eyes were so scared. I'd been doing hedge magic all my life. Bringing back plants, doing the odd luck spell. It's why my cooking is so good. So in that moment, I just . . . acted. Said the words to a spell I'd done a hundred times to make my petunias bloom."

Clearing her throat, she reached into her handbag and pulled out a tissue. As she dabbed at her eyes, Nana said, "And then you were back. Just like that. Killed every plant within a ten-block radius, but you were back. So I put my silver bracelet on you, and I . . . I hoped." She nodded at the bracelet. "That's what anchors the spell, what anchors your soul in your body."

"But it wasn't enough," I said softly, remembering Maya just that evening, bringing our basil plant back to life.

Nana gave a little laugh. "No, it wasn't. A human soul is a powerful thing, Izzy. It takes so much power to hold it. And no matter how many plants or birds or stray dogs I drained, it was like I could feel Dex's soul flickering. So I looked to other spell books, tried other rituals."

"And ended up summoning a really pissed-off ghost."

"An unfortunate side effect," she sniffed. "But really,

I've just been delaying the inevitable. Until an entire human life force is drained off, given to Dex, his existence is just . . . temporary."

Finally I understood what I'd sensed when I had touched Dex. No wonder he'd felt both magic and non-magic. Magic was keeping him alive. In his own way, he was a ghost. Or a zombie. Which meant I'd kissed . . .

No, definitely a ghost.

Dex was shaking his head and blinking, backing away from his Nana. "No," he said, hands trembling. "No, no, no, that is not possible. I can't be dead, and this"—he hooked one finger under his bracelet— "can't be the only thing keeping me alive."

Nana calmly regarded him through her glasses. "Take it off, then."

"No!" I cried, as Dex started to tug at the silver around his wrist. But he froze, finger coiled around the metal. "I can't."

"Compulsion spell," Nana said. "I didn't want to risk anything."

Knees giving out, Dex sunk to the floor, head in one hand. "No," he said, but I could see a tear splash down into the salt. When he lifted his face, his eyes were red. "Nana, how could you do something like . . ." Trailing off, he looked at Romy, crumpled and sobbing, clearly in pain. "That's because of me. Mr. Snyder, a–and Beth

Tanner, and the gym. And now Romy, the first friend I made at that stupid school, is possessed by a freaking vengeful ghost that you summoned because you were so busy trying to keep me alive."

Dex was crying, but he got up off the floor, dusting the salt from his pin-striped pants. "I'm not letting that happen. If I die, will this stop? Will the-the energy or whatever is powering the ghost shut down?"

Behind him, Maya shook her head no, but Dex was already tugging at his bracelet again. "Because I'll take this off. If me dying means that Romy can be okay, then I'm fine with that. Apparently I've been living on borrowed time anyway."

His whole body was shaking, but he held his chin high and his gaze was steady. He would do it, I had no doubt.

Nana stepped forward, trying to cup his face, but he flinched from her touch. "No, sweet boy," she said gently. "This isn't all your fault. It's mine. I just . . ." Her voice wavered, and this time, when she tried to touch him, Dex let her, albeit reluctantly. "I just loved you so much. And I'm so sorry I've hurt people, but I'm so glad I got this extra year with you."

Confused, Dex shook his head, but Nana was already moving toward Romy. Kneeling down, she patted Romy's hair and then reached into her handbag and pulled out a tiny blade. I stepped forward, but Maya caught my arm.

In a series of quick moves, Nana sliced an X into her palm and laid her bloody hand on Romy's back. Then she smiled at Dex. "I love you," she told him.

Dex, still shaking, only stared at her.

Nana looked to Romy, who had flickered back to Mary. "I'm sorry," she told her. "I should have let you rest. I had no idea what had really been done to you, or how angry you were."

"Nana—" Dex said, but she just ducked her head and whispered something. The light that filled the cave was blinding and sudden, and came with a concussive boom that made us all stagger backward.

When I could finally see again, Romy was sitting up, blearily shaking her head while Anderson knelt down next to her. "Um, ow," she murmured, and it was so clearly Romy—only Romy—that a sudden sob of relief welled up in my throat.

But then there was another sob. Dex was on his knees by his Nana. Her eyes were closed and she was smiling slightly, but there was no doubt she was gone.

He lifted his tearstained face to me and Maya. "What happened?"

Maya shook her head. "I'm not sure. I've never heard that spell she used before." Crouching down, she gently lifted Dex's hand from Nana's back. His shoulders were heaving, and I wanted to say something, do something, but I had no idea where to start.

Without warning, Maya flicked the clasp on Dex's bracelet and I darted forward, hand out. "Maya!"

The bracelet fell harmlessly to the ground, but Dex stayed right where he was. Still breathing—well, wheezing actually. He fished his inhaler out of his pocket and jammed it into his mouth, eyes on the bracelet.

Once his breathing sounded normal again, Maya laid a hand on his shoulder. "That's what I thought. She knew that the only way to stop Mary was for her to die. But whatever that spell was, it didn't just kill her, it . . . transferred her. Put her life energy into you."

Dex lowered the inhaler. "So, I'm . . . not going to die?"

Shrugging, Maya picked up the bracelet and pressed it into Dex's palm. "Well, eventually you will, just like we all will. But not today." With that, she pulled Dex into a hug.

In shock, Dex raised his arms almost numbly and draped them around her neck.

"Nana did the right thing in the end," Maya said. "And she did it for you."

If Dex replied, I couldn't hear it.

CHAPTER 33

"So, you were . . . dead."

"Romy," I warned, but she just shrugged and pulled the blanket tighter around her.

"Look, I get that he's traumatized, but hey, I am, too."

"We all are," Anderson muttered.

The four of us were sitting in my living room, Romy and Anderson huddled on the couch, me in the one recliner we had, and Dex at my feet, his arms wrapped around his knees, a blanket over his shoulders. He hadn't said anything since we'd left the cave.

But now he looked at Romy, and a ghost of his old grin crossed his face. "Yeah, I was. And *still* better looking than any of the other guys at Mary Evans High." His voice wavered a little at the end, and he went back to chewing his thumbnail. I wanted to lay my hand on top of his head or pat his back. Something. Instead, I crossed my arms over my chest.

"So he was dead," Romy reiterated, nodding at Dex. "And you"—she looked at me—"you're some kind of awesome monster slayer."

"I don't feel so awesome right now," I muttered. Maybe because no monsters had been slain. Sure, we'd stopped the hedge witch and brought an end to the hauntings, but this didn't feel even a little bit like winning. Not when I looked at Dex's shattered expression. His Nana hadn't been evil. Just wrong. And to be honest, I wondered if she'd even been that. What would I have done to bring Finley back if I could've? Or my mom if something happened to her? When you don't have much family left, you'll do anything to protect what you have.

The front door opened and we all jumped, but it was just Maya.

Dex stood up as she came in. "You took care of her?" he asked. "You didn't just . . . leave her there?"

Maya had stayed behind at the cave to, in her words, "put things to rights." Now she patted Dexter's arm, sympathy written all over her broad face. "I did. With respect. She was a sister, and we have ways of handling these things."

Confused, Dex stared at her. "A sis— Oh, right,

because you were both witches. Because that's real. That's a thing that really happens, and my Nana was one."

He went back to sitting and chewing.

Letting him have a moment, I turned to Romy and Anderson. "So if it was Dex's Nana accidentally raising ghosts, why was your charm in that cave?" I asked Romy.

Grimacing, she took another sip of the tea Maya had made. "I told you, I have no idea. I lost the stupid thing."

From the other end of the couch, Anderson cleared his throat. "Um . . . I might actually know why. I took the charm."

Romy's blanket slipped off her shoulders as she sat up. "You what? Why?"

Anderson's face was bright red, matching the plaid throw draped around him. "I saw this thing on the Internet about doing a . . . a love spell." He mumbled the last words so much that it sounded like he said, "abub-smell."

"You did a love spell on me?" Romy said, her "me" becoming a shriek.

"Yes!" Anderson said, tossing the blanket off and getting up to pace the living room. "And I know that's awful, and I shouldn't have, but . . . I liked you, and I thought it couldn't hurt." He hung his head a little. "So that's why we kissed at the graveyard that night. I'm sorry."

Huh. So Dex and I hadn't been the only ones using our PMS field trip romantically.

Romy slugged Anderson on the shoulder. "You idiot," she cried. "Did you do the love spell in eighth grade?"

"What? No. I did it, like, last month."

"Well, eighth grade is when I started liking you," Romy said, hitting him again. "So no, it wasn't the love spell that made me kiss you in the graveyard. And it's not the love spell making me kiss you now."

With that, she grabbed the front of his shirt and yanked his mouth down to hers.

It had been an awful night. A night so full of bad, even Everton and Leslie would've shuddered, and they had once spent a night getting chased by a serial killer on a train. But seeing Romy and Anderson kiss, I smiled. They were safe and happy, and that had to be worth something.

Looking over at Dex, I saw that he was smiling, too. Our eyes met, and I wondered if he was thinking the same thing.

The four of us, plus Maya, sat there for another hour or so before Romy and Anderson decided they should head home. As they walked to the door, I stopped Romy. "Look, I'm sorry about—"

She pulled me into a hug before I had time to finish. "I'm sorry, too."

I wrapped my arms tight around her, hugging her back, and when she pulled away, I hoped she wouldn't see the tears in my eyes. "I'm probably going to take tomorrow off from school," she said. "And you should, too. Maybe you could come over? See if Leslie survives that polar bear attack?"

My throat tightened, but I made myself nod. "Sure. I'd like that."

Once they were gone, Maya went into the kitchen, ostensibly to make some more tea, but really to give me and Dex some alone time, I think.

I counted sixteen of my own heartbeats before he said, "She won't see you tomorrow, will she?"

There was no sense in lying. "No. As soon as my mom gets back, we'll leave."

"And do what?" he asked, looking up at me. "Go to some other town? Fight some other evil?"

"Your Nana wasn't evil, Dex," I said, but he shook his head.

"You know what I mean."

I sighed. "Yeah. We will."

Standing up, clutching the blanket in front of him, Dex met my eyes. "Great. Because I'm coming with you."

"Dex," I said, but he cut me off.

"Look, I know you have to do the big hero thing

of, 'no, I must work alone, my love for you can only be a hindrance,' but . . . Izzy, what else am I supposed to do?" His voice quavered. "My parents are dead. My Nana is . . . is dead. And magic and monsters are apparently *real*. I can't just forget that. And I get that if you more or less adopt me, that will make things weird for us, but we don't have to be . . . We could just be friends."

I looked into Dex's blue eyes, remembering how brave he'd been. He'd been willing to die to save Romy's life, willing to do it in an instant. He might not be able to run or fight, but Dex had the biggest heart of anyone I knew. And I needed that. I needed him.

"I think there may be a friend-shaped spot for you, yeah," I said softly, and he smiled.

"But first—" I hesitated, chewing my lower lip. "I . . . I need to show you something."

Turning, I led Dex down the hall to the guest room.

I paused with my hand on the doorknob. "What I'm about to show you, it . . . it's pretty weird," I warned him.

"Oh, right, because everything else that happened tonight was totally typical." He was going for quippy, but there were tears streaking his cheeks and his voice sounded shaky.

Normally, I would've smiled at his attempt at humor, but what I was about to do was too big for smiling, and

Dex must've sensed that. "Sorry," he said, laying a hand on my arm. "I just mean . . . whatever weirdness there is, I'm prepared for it."

I didn't think there was any way he could be, but I nodded. "Okay, then."

Torin's mirror was covered up when I opened the door, but I could hear him as he said, "Ah, you're back! All hail the conquering hero."

Dex paused in the doorway. "Who was that?"

"You're braced for weird, right?" I asked, moving toward the mirror.

He visibly swallowed, but after a second, Dex nodded. "Braced. Weird. Bring it."

I pulled the canvas down from the mirror, and there stood Torin, leaning against the bed as always. Dex glanced back and forth between the bed in the mirror and the bed in the room before letting out a slow breath. "Okay. Yeah, that is . . . that is weird, all right."

"Who the sodding hell is this?" Torin narrowed his eyes. "Oh, right. That boy who plays all the video games. The one Isolde fancies."

"Torin," I said warningly, but Dex smiled a little even as his eyes roamed over Torin's mirror.

"Oi," Torin snapped. "Fancy-dress boy, my eyes are up here."

Dex met those eyes, one corner of his mouth still

lifted in a half-grin. "'Fancy-dress boy?' This from a dude who dresses like Prince?"

I snorted with laughter and Torin scowled. "Prince who?"

Then Dex laughed, too, and after a while, the sound actually sounded normal and not choked with tears.

"I do not like him," Torin declared, pointing at Dex. "I disapprove of your choice of paramour *immensely*."

"He's not my paramour," I said, rolling my eyes. "He's my friend."

"Right," Dex said, finally letting the blanket slip from his shoulders. Rolling them as though he were free of a great weight, he looked down at me and stuck his hand out. "Friends."

We shook on it, and there was no tingle of magic this time. But that didn't mean I didn't feel anything. Dex's eyes held mine and I knew I should pull my hand back, but suddenly that was the last thing I wanted to do.

"I am going to be sick," Torin muttered, turning away. "Completely, riotously sick right here in the mirror; and let me tell you, that is *quite* a mess."

"So is this." Dex and I both turned to see Mom in the doorway, but before I could say anything, she strode in, a hammer raised high in one fist. With a shriek, we jumped apart as Mom brought the hammer down as hard as she could on Torin's mirror.

CHAPTER 34

"**M**om!" I cried as a few shards flew up, making tiny scratches along Mom's arms. But she didn't seem to feel them. Torin staggered backward, and in the mirror, the table teetered, nearly falling.

For four hundred years, Torin had aggravated and frustrated Brannicks, but he'd always been a part of our lives. I'd always assumed there was some kind of rule that we couldn't hurt him. After all, if he could be destroyed, wouldn't someone have done it by now, to heck with prophecies?

The frame shook, and Torin grimaced. Or at least I thought he did. It was hard to tell what was going on in all those fractured pieces.

Mom stood there, breathing hard, the hammer raised. Blood dripped down her arms, but she didn't seem to notice it. I waited for the glass to fall out of the frame, for Torin to become nothing more than a handful of shards.

There was no flash of light or smell of smoke. None of the stuff you expect when magic is happening around you. Just a soft *pop!* and suddenly Torin was complete again. The glass wasn't even scratched, much less cracked.

"That was uncalled for," he said, straightening his jerkin.

"You lied to me," Mom growled. "You told me you had seen Finley, and then sent me on a wild-goose chase while Izzy nearly got killed."

Her gaze moved to me, her face full of anger and worry and something else I couldn't name.

"*He* was your source?" I asked, pointing at Torin. "You're always telling me not to trust him, and—"

"With good reason," Mom said, and now I understood what was in her voice. She was angry not just with Torin, but with herself.

"Izzy needed a chance to spread her wings, Aislinn," Torin said, giving a bored shrug. "And you needed to get out of her way. She handled herself masterfully tonight. Proved to be a true Brannick."

Mom watched him for a long time. "She's always been a true Brannick," she said at last. Then she strode forward and grabbed the canvas, covering Torin. "We're done," she said, more to herself than anyone else. "We should've been done with him a long time ago."

She turned back, and for the first time seemed to notice Dex. "Who is this?"

"I'm Dexter O'Neil, Mrs. Brannick," Dex said, offering his hand to shake. "And I'm hoping you'll adopt me."

Mom looked back and forth between the two of us before muttering, "I need a drink," and walking out of the room.

In the silence that followed, I raised an eyebrow at Dex. "So . . . this is my family. Sure you want in?"

Dex looked back and forth between the door and Torin's mirror. "My Nana was a witch who kept me alive by raising evil ghosts. The bar for family dysfunction has already been set pretty high."

Half an hour later, we all sat at the kitchen table—me, Dex, Mom, and Maya. I told Mom everything that had happened at the cave. When I got to the part about Maya handing me the knife, she looked up. "Would you have killed her?" she asked. "If it meant destroying the ghost?"

I thought about it, turning my cup of tea around in my hands. "I don't know," I finally said. I knew it probably wasn't the answer Mom wanted, but it was the honest one. "I don't think so. I think I would've tried to find some other way, no matter what."

To my surprise, Mom smiled and reached out. She didn't quite tousle my hair—her hand moved too roughly for that—but it was an affectionate gesture nonetheless. "You're a good kid, Izzy," she said. "Sometimes that's what being a Brannick means. It's not always about storming in and saving the day yourself. It's about the willingness to do whatever it takes to keep people safe. I still don't like that Torin lied to me—especially about Finn—but—"

"I don't like him either," Dex said, speaking up for the first time since we'd sat down. "Both for lying to you, and just sort of on general principle. For the record."

The corner of Mom's mouth lifted in a half smile. "Good to know. So what are we supposed to do with you, Dexter O'Neil?"

Dex leaned back in his chair, trying to affect that super-casual thing he usually did so well. But his hands were shaking and his face looked ravaged. "Well, I may not have superpowers, and it's true my asthma may get in the way of much monster chasing, but I did used to be dead, and I faced down a terrifying ghost tonight. So, I'd like to . . . join your gang. Or whatever. There aren't any initiation rituals involving blood, are there?" He shuddered, and Mom cut her eyes at me.

I gave a little shrug.

"You understand why I might be hesitant to let my daughter's boyfriend move in with us, right?"

"I'm not her boyfriend," Dex said, his voice

completely serious. "I'm just her friend. I swear." He lifted his hand in what I think was supposed to be a Boy Scout salute but just ended up looking like a vaguely obscene gesture.

Mom turned back to me. "That true, Iz? This guy is nothing more than a friend?"

I looked at Dex and ignored the twisting in my heart. He was right. So we had liked each other. We could get over that. Especially if it meant Dex could stay with us.

"It is," I told her.

Sighing, Mom stood up and braced her hands on her lower back. "Well, we've solved Ideal's ghost problem. So where to next?"

Maya leaned back in her seat. "I have at least three file folders for you to look through. Couple of interesting cases just came in over the last few weeks."

Mom nodded. "Good. And there's another thing." She laid both hands on the table, leaning in so that she could meet my eyes. "Yes, the research I've been doing is about Finley. I've been trying to track the history of the coven Finn was with the night she disappeared, reading up on other vanishings, seeing if there's anything, any scrap that can help us find her. And I didn't tell you because I . . ." She looked down, flexing her fingers. "I didn't want to get your hopes up if it all came to nothing."

I reached out and covered her hand with my own. "Mom, knowing is better than not knowing every time, okay?"

After a moment, she squeezed back. "Okay." Then, slapping her palms on the table, she straightened up. "So we have more monsters to fight, places to go, and your sister to find. We have our work cut out for us."

Clearing his throat, Dex leaned forward and raised his eyebrows. "And does that 'we' include me?"

Mom looked down at me, and I could read the question in her eyes. If I said yes, she'd let Dex come with us. Which would mean traveling with Dex. *Living* with Dex.

But that would be fine. So we'd kissed a few times. It wasn't like we'd had some long-lasting relationship or anything. Surely downgrading to "just friends" and, basically, "work partners" would be easy enough. No matter how blue his eyes were.

I gave Mom the tiniest nod, and she returned it.

Putting one hand on Dex's shoulder, Mom gave him a little shake, making him wince. "Welcome to the Brannick family, Dexter."

Acknowledgments

Massive thanks to my editor, Catherine Onder, for all the hard work she put into making Izzy, Dex, Torin, and Company be the best and shiniest they could be! Also thanks to Lisa Yoskowitz for taking such good care of me and the book; and to Hayley Wagreich for being such a freaking Wonder Girl.

As always, thanks to my Agent of Amazingness, Holly Root, without whom none of my books would ever have been written, much less published.

Hugs and tea for Victoria Schwab, who claimed Dex as her own roughly five minutes after she read his first scene, so sorry, ladies (and Izzy).

Thanks to everyone at Disney-Hyperion for giving me and my books such a lovely home over the years.

Big, big thanks to all of my family and friends, who put up with me when I lock myself in a room for days, muttering things like, "But how would you kill a ghost?" Y'all are the bestest and I love you.

And to all of my readers: thank you, thank you, thank you. You're all lovely and amazing, and I'm so lucky to have each and every one of you.